# HERE GHOST NOTHING

A REAPER WITCH MYSTERY: BOOK 9

ELLE ADAMS

This book was written, produced and edited in the UK, where some spelling, grammar and word usage will vary from US English.

Copyright © 2023 Elle Adams
All rights reserved.

To be notified when Elle Adams's next book is released, sign up to her author newsletter.

1

Eight days remained until Halloween, and I was starting to think that fending off the apocalypse would be more doable than dealing with a legion of ghosts on the spookiest night of the year.

"Who are they?" I asked my ghostly brother, Mart, indicating the group of transparent figures who'd just floated into the restaurant in which I worked.

"Haven't a clue." The pumpkin-shaped hat he'd taken to wearing bobbed up and down as he spoke. Since he was invisible to most people except for me and Jia, my coworker, the pumpkin gave the restaurant's customers some warning whenever he decided to lurk near their tables and rearrange their cutlery for a prank.

"Ghost tourists. Wonderful." I shook my head. "Do they have any idea that this place might be the site of Armageddon in less than two weeks?"

Mart shrugged and resumed drifting through the restaurant, rattling plates and generally living up to his reputation as the inn's most annoying spirit-in-residence. Which was saying something, given the entire town of Hawkwood Hollow was a veritable haven for ghosts.

"Something up, Maura?" My boss, Allie, came striding over, her hat jangling with bat-shaped ornaments. It probably said something about the state of the inn that her shimmering purple cloak didn't stand out amidst the general Halloween décor. Every customer ended up covered in pumpkin-shaped glitter or fake cobwebs within a moment of stepping through the door.

"We have some new ghosts," I replied. "I think they heard about the event and wanted to join in."

Her expression relaxed into a smile. "I'm glad word is spreading."

*No surprise.* I was pretty sure Allie and her teenage daughter Carey had taken out ads in every magical publication within their budget, and evidently, the local spirits had their own gossip networks as well. Everyone in the vicinity knew that on Halloween, the Riverside Inn was the place to be.

There was just one small problem: namely, that the leader of the local witch coven was missing, captured by her predecessor, who'd announced that she intended to use Halloween to unleash some nefarious plan. Not that Allie and Carey would let the small matter of an oncoming apocalypse prevent them from giving their guests a night to remember.

Jia ducked behind the counter, back from delivering a tray of Halloween-themed cocktails to a nearby table. "New ghosts?"

"Tourists, by the looks of things." I side-eyed the transparent newcomers. "You'd think the sage would put them off."

Our anticipation of an attack by Mina Devlin had led us to scatter sage all over the area outside the inn. Sage repelled spirits, and it also repelled any nasties from the afterworld that Mina and her allies might unleash on us. We'd especially been watching the river that ran through the centre of Hawkwood Hollow and the tunnels beneath the bridge from which the last attack had come.

"You'd think," Jia said. "Well... I might have heard some of them saying the inn is the safest place in the area."

I groaned inwardly. "Let me guess: they think I'm cooking up a plan to beat Mina?"

*I wish.* I'd certainly been *trying* to figure out how to stop our rogue coven leader, but nobody knew where she was hiding, much less what she planned to do on the night when the barriers between the realms of living and dead would be thinner than usual. That was Halloween, more commonly referred to as "Samhain" in the witching world. Her attempts to bargain with demons for power had caused the river to burst its banks two decades ago and was the reason Hawkwood Hollow was inhabited by more ghosts than living people. Yet she'd failed, ultimately, thanks to the local Reaper's bid to stop her.

Now she wanted to try something similar again, and everyone seemed to think *I'd* be the one to stop her this time. It was an awful lot of pressure to put on one ex-Reaper who didn't even own a scythe.

"They trust you," said Jia. "Come on. You have to admit that you've got the better of her before."

I grunted. "I think running an amazing ghost tour *and* stopping Armageddon in the same night might be too much to ask."

Allie and Carey had spent the past few months planning the inn's biggest ghostly extravaganza, and postponing it until after Halloween would be a disaster for their business. I'd been sure that we'd manage to find Mina beforehand—or that she wouldn't be able to resist striking first—but as the days trickled by, my hopes had begun to dim.

"It's not all on you," said Jia. "We're all trying to search for Mina's hiding place. The police have been out there almost every day."

I grimaced. "I know. Drew says that there have been a dozen false alarms, but either she's moving between locations every other day, or she's using some kind of concealment spell that can muddle even a shifter's senses."

Mina had ample resources at her disposal, including the current head of the coven, assuming Jennifer was still alive by this point—it wouldn't have surprised me if Mina had forced her prisoner to assist her.

"Yeah." Jia grabbed a cloth and wiped yet more Halloween-themed glitter off the counter. "I guess Mina's hiding somewhere no tracking spell can find."

"Nor any Reaper." Few things could block my Reaper abilities, but Mina had been busy figuring out ways to achieve the impossible. The last time we'd clashed, the scythe I'd borrowed from the local Reaper had bounced clean off her.

"You'd think the Reaper Council would be chasing her down," Jia remarked. "She's torn up their rule book and stomped all over the pieces."

"If they have been, they haven't told me." I spoke in a low voice. "I wish I knew how she's running circles around them. That's what I was hoping to find in the library."

I'd taken a brief excursion away from Hawkwood Hollow to visit a library that contained what was supposed to be the biggest store of magical knowledge in the whole of the UK, but I'd come back without any concrete answers as to how Mina had managed to both repel my Reaper skills *and* get her hands on a book that was supposed to be the property of the Council. Granted, the latter was likely not a piece of information the Reaper Council wanted to broadcast across the country.

"It was worth looking anyway," Jia said. "And Carey was happy with the footage you brought back from those vampires' creepy house."

"Vampires." I gave a shudder. "I'd be surprised if they didn't have a role in how she robbed the Reapers."

To say Reapers and vampires didn't get along was like saying the north of England was a bit rainy. Vamps and Reapers were more or less equally matched skill-wise, but each had their own advantages, and the vampires' included thousands of years of accumulated knowledge and an immunity to Reapers. Which Mina had now conveniently acquired. *Hmm.*

"Ask your dad," said Jia. "I know you've been avoiding paying him a visit."

"She's right, you know," added Mart.

"You don't want to visit him either," I pointed out. "Because you know Mum would notice if we showed up at our old town."

I could guarantee that going to my parents' hometown of Greenwood Lake wouldn't bring me any answers, either—just another source of stress that I didn't need.

"Isn't your mother a coven leader?" Jia queried. "I know you probably don't want to put her in Mina's crosshairs…"

"Oh, Mina won't know my mother's coven exists." No, the quiver of dread that arose at the thought of paying a visit to my old home was for another reason entirely. "Greenwood Lake is a nonentity even by the magical world's standards, and they certainly don't have any supersecret ways to defeat Mina."

Jia propped a hand on her hip. "But your dad knows the Reaper Council. Isn't it worth a try?"

He did, but I was treading a fine line with the Council already. With every Reaper I met, I risked someone coming into Hawkwood Hollow and deciding to banish every ghost in town, little knowing that they'd be playing into Mina's hands if they did so. More to the point, the ghosts *lived* here, and the Reaper Council had no right to play landlord and boot them out.

"I don't want to run off at a time when you need us," I protested. "It's nearly Halloween."

Jia raised an eyebrow at me. "Is that the only problem? The inn will be quiet tomorrow, you know. No ghost tours."

"It'll still be Monday." The inn's busiest periods depended on when we were running ghost tours, but we'd been booked solid all month. Those who hadn't been able to secure a room had opted to stay in nearby towns and pay visits to the restaurant every other day, and I expected to end up having to turn people away by the end of next week.

"Allie and I will handle things," she said. "I think you should go and visit home. Right, Allie?"

"Yes?" Allie herself came over with her arms laden with what appeared to be inflatable ghost costumes. "Which of you ordered these?"

"Maura should go see her parents," said Jia. "She's been coming up with excuses for weeks. And I don't know who ordered them. Maura?"

"No," I replied. "And no, this isn't urgent enough. I can see my parents anytime."

*Or not, if Armageddon actually does happen next week.*

Mart sprang up behind me and blew on the back of my neck. "That might not be true."

"I didn't think you wanted to see them either." My brother had an even-more fraught relationship with our parents than I did. They'd reacted in different ways to his untimely death, and neither had been positive.

As the living person caught in the middle, I'd caused controversy enough myself when I'd brought him back as a ghost and tethered him to me, which was not a way in which an apprentice was supposed to apply their Reaper powers. While Dad and I had recently reconciled, Mum was a different story, and my extended family on her side had blamed the Reapers for Mart's death. Including me.

"I don't," Mart replied. "But we already saw Dad, and the coven ought to have forgotten we exist by now."

"Forgotten we exist?" My phone chimed a message. I slid it out of my pocket and was greeted with an inexplicable *Your package has been delivered* message, topped with an image of the inflatable ghost costumes Allie had just dropped off at the counter. "What—did *you* use my phone to order ghost costumes?"

Mart snickered in answer.

"Are you talking to your brother?" Allie guessed. "If you want to take a half day to visit home, it's not a problem. You've worked back-to-back shifts ever since you got back from your last trip."

"I know, but... Mart, stop that."

Mart picked up one of the ghost costumes, causing the others to slide into a pile on the floor. "Do you think this suits me?"

"You're unbelievable." I caught Jia hiding a grin. "You didn't encourage him, did you?"

"I didn't need to." She crouched to help Allie pick up the costumes. "Seriously. Go home. Bond with your parents. It worked with your dad."

*That was different.* I turned to Mart and whispered, "Do you actually think he'll let us in on the Reaper Council's secrets? We certainly don't want *them* to know you exist."

"They don't have to know. I can be stealthy." He lifted the inflatable ghost costume into the air, almost knocking several glasses over in the process. "Besides, it'll be fun to see how Mum reacts to that boyfriend of yours."

*I'm going to regret this,* I thought as I left the inn the following morning. Mart floated at my side—thankfully, minus the inflatable ghost costume—whistling the theme from *Doctor Who*. I had no idea where his sudden desire to go back home had come from, unless he really did think Dad had been concocting a scheme to stop Mina with the help of the Reaper Council and hadn't let us know.

Actually, that wouldn't be out of character for Dad. He was as committed to secrecy as any Reaper I'd met, but I was sure that nobody knew how to stop Mina. Not even him.

In any case, I'd caved and agreed to take the morning off work for an unpleasant trip down memory lane. Drew had offered to come with me, but I'd figured my mother would be shaken enough at my sudden appearance without me bringing a new boyfriend with me as well. Let alone a new boyfriend who happened to be a werewolf and the head of the police in a town that was infested with ghosts. Oh, and that said town might be the target of a megalomaniac witch's power play in a few days. *And instead of dealing with that, I'm going back to a place that was more than happy to see the back of me.*

"Are you sure about this?" I pulled out my wand. "Do you really want to visit the same coven members who started a magical duel at your funeral?"

"They don't have to know we're there," Mart said. "Not if we transport ourselves in and out again without anyone else seeing us."

"Transportation spells don't work inside the coven headquarters," I reminded him. "And we'd scare Mum to death if we appeared out of the afterworld in her office."

"It'd be funny to see her face." Mart snickered to himself. "You want to see her first, then? Not Dad?"

"I say we get the hard bit over with first." That and if we visited Mum first, there was less chance of her popping up at the Reaper's house when we were talking to Dad. I really *didn't* want her to know about Mina Devlin.

*Get the hard bit over with. Right.* "All right. Let's go in."

In a flick of my wand, the inn disappeared, to be replaced with a country hillside that wasn't overly different from the one we'd left behind. Neither was the cluster of small buildings that lay in the dip between two of the larger hills, bordered by the blue expanse that gave Greenwood Lake its name. Several buildings sat upon an island within the lake, and I surveyed them, taking in a deep breath.

"The house is still there." Mart spoke from behind me, having mercifully abandoned his plan to scare the hell out of Mum and appear in her home. "Aren't you coming?"

"Yes." As soon as we'd touched down on the hillside, all the bad memories had come swarming back, and it took all my willpower not to turn away.

"Don't go getting cold feet." Mart prodded me in the back, creating the sensation of someone tipping ice cubes down the back of my shirt. "Look, hardly anyone's outside on a dismal day like this."

"True." The murky, overcast sky was a blessing, really. "Okay. Showtime."

I descended the hill, skirting the cluster of buildings, and made for the dock at the edge of the lake. My mother's mounting paranoia had led her to set up anti-trespasser spells all around the lake, with the result that the only way to reach the island in the centre was to use one of the coven's boats. I hadn't tested to see whether my Reaper skills could get around that boundary, but the one time I had tried a transportation spell to get in, I'd ended up being thrown headfirst into the lake.

"You don't need to act like we're on our way to a funeral."

Mart hovered above one of the small boats docked at the lakeside.

"We might as well be." I climbed into the boat, which began moving by itself. Handy, admittedly, but the feeling of being trapped only intensified while the boat carried us to the centre of the lake. Nobody was outside, but curious faces peered from the windows, and I could practically hear the rumours fizzing in the air.

I ducked my head. While I wished I'd worn a disguise, any witch who could see spirits would have spotted Mart, too, and he had no intention of hiding. I had to shush his increasingly high-pitched singing when the boat halted at the island, and we climbed out onto the muddy shore.

The cluster of houses upon the island hadn't changed a bit in the past few years, especially the central Victorian-style mansion of red brick with flowers blooming at every window. Not a single Halloween decoration in sight, but Mum was fairly traditional as far as coven leaders went. There'd be a Samhain parade on the actual night, but no inflatable ghosts or pumpkins marred the tasteful décor.

With trepidation, I rapped on the door.

My mother answered, dressed in her usual green-cloak-and-hat ensemble. People would have said we looked alike, with our blue eyes and dark hair and pale skin, though she wasn't half-Reaper, so her hair was shinier and her eyes brighter than mine. With tears. Uh-oh.

"Maura!" she wailed, flinging her arms around me.

This was going to end well.

"Mum… don't cry." I awkwardly patted her shoulder. "Sorry I didn't let you know in advance. I… misplaced my contacts list."

"I called you every day!"

*I know. That was why I changed my phone number.* It was impossible to live any kind of life with her messaging me every hour to ask for the minute details of my day. Between that and Mart's relentless ghostly presence causing me to end up turfed out of every job or town I tried to settle in, something had had to give.

Now I was going to pay for those months of silence. With a martyr-like air, I followed Mum into the coven headquarters. Mart tried to drift away, but I beckoned him with a crooked finger. He wasn't getting out of this one that easily, and I needed him here to create a diversion in case the rest of the coven decided to shove their noses in.

Mum led me into her office and promptly collapsed into tears. I gave her ten minutes of sobbing recriminations before I put my foot down.

"Mum, I called and left you a message with my new address whenever I moved house. You might have visited at any time." Granted, I hadn't done so with Hawkwood Hollow, but I hadn't initially expected to stay.

"I can't leave the coven!" She fumbled for a handkerchief. "It's inconceivable. Your aunt Rosie would have gone snooping in my office."

*You could just fire her, you know.* I bit back the comment and gave a shrug. "It was just a suggestion."

"Oh, it'd be different if I had a successor." She sniffed. "If you'd stayed…"

*And there it is.* "Mum, you know why I couldn't stay here."

"You might have been coven leader!" Her eyes brightened with tears again. "I'd have trained you myself."

"I was never going to be a coven leader." I'd already turned away from that path when I'd taken on an apprenticeship as a Reaper, and while Mum had adjusted to that decision eventually, it'd all changed with Mart's death. She seemed to have forgotten that our extended family had kicked me out of the coven while she'd been mired in grief.

As Mum's sobbing intensified, I scrambled for a distraction. "I'm seeing someone," I blurted. "Romantically."

"What?" Her sobs cut off in a gasp. "You never told me. When did you meet?"

I might have told her if she had let me get a word in edgeways. "I'm living in a town called Hawkwood Hollow. Drew's the head of the local police force there. We met..." *At a crime scene* was the honest answer.

"What Hollow?" Mum jumped in without noticing that I'd omitted the end of that sentence. "Doesn't sound familiar."

"It's kind of... small." To say the least. "But I've been living there for a few months now, and everything's going great."

"You'll have to bring him here!" she insisted. "What did you say his name was? Drew?"

"Ah... he's busy, but maybe one weekend, we can come over." If I could get her to drop her insistence at trying to convince me to move back home again. I did not need her sobbing in front of Drew, aka one of the myriad reasons I hadn't wanted to come back.

"We have to make up for lost time!" she said. "Drew's the head of the police, is he? He must have some stories."

"Mm." I made a noncommittal noise. "He's busy. So am I, for that matter. I work at—"

"Work!" She exclaimed. "What work? You never said you had a job."

"I thought it was implied." I wasn't exactly rolling in cash, as she ought to have known, and most of my previous jobs had been short-lived, courtesy of Mart's ghostly presence. "I work at an inn and restaurant."

"Customer service?" Her brow wrinkled. "You must hate that."

"It's not bad." *Okay, time to end this conversation.* "Mart likes it too."

I put a slight emphasis on his name, raising my voice, and a window slammed upstairs in response.

Mum lifted her head. "Oh, is that your brother?"

"Yes." *And my cue to leave.* "Tell you what, you two can catch up. I was going to drop by to see Dad too. Then I have to get back to work."

Mart descended through the ceiling, knocking a stack of paperwork off Mum's desk. "Aunt Rosie's as nice as ever. She swore a blue streak when I locked her office door."

Mum leapt to her feet to pick up the papers. "Oh, you didn't, did you?"

"At least it means she's not bothering us," I said. "She might be family, but she's a weasel. Actually, that might be insulting to weasels."

Mum gave a sound halfway between a sob and a laugh. "I've missed you, Maura. You know, it wouldn't be difficult for you to move back here. I can find you somewhere to live right away. Both of you."

*Not a chance.* "I told you I'm not working for *any* coven. I like the inn. We're busy preparing for Halloween, which is why we're busy over the next few weeks—"

"Samhain, you mean?" She straightened upright, pushing the papers back into place. "Why, is it a hotel for witches?"

"No... erm. It's haunted." I gestured to Mart. "Mart, come over here and tell Mum all about the inn."

Mum's eyes brimmed over with tears again. "Oh... of course. You must be so lonely!"

Mart tutted and rolled his eyes. "Lonely!"

"Mart." I marched over to him and whispered, "Distract her. If you do, I'll let you use the shower tonight."

"He still likes hot showers!" Mum sobbed even harder, having heard the end of my whisper. *Great.* Honestly, when she was in this kind of mood, every word I said was liable to set her off.

"Yes, he does," I told her. "He's *fine*, Mum, and so am I. Anyway, I need to see Dad."

Mart gave a long-suffering sigh and then drifted over to Mum. "I'm not lonely. The inn has approximately a hundred ghosts living in it. And I'm the best of all."

*That ought to distract her.* While Mart began an exaggerated spiel about our ghost-tour business, I managed to extricate myself from the conversation by promising to call this time and left the coven headquarters for my second unwelcome visit of the day.

## 2

One boat ride later, I reached the lake's edge. By some miracle, no other coven members had accosted me on the way out, though I figured Mart had either entertained or terrified them into submission. Hoping it was the latter, I climbed the hill until I came to a house that stood apart from the others.

Dad's house was about what you'd expect from a Reaper: large, grand, and entirely unsuited for the modern day. A chill swept outward when he answered the door. He was a quintessential Reaper, too: tall with dark hair and pale, pale skin. He wore a perpetually tired expression that only intensified when he looked at me.

"I should have expected you to show up here soon," he said. "Where's your brother?"

"Distracting Mum." He did acknowledge Mart's existence now, but at the mention of Mum, he gave a faint sigh.

We entered the sitting room—well, "sitting" was a relative term, since Reapers were more into looming in corners, looking creepy. The hard-backed wooden chairs that existed for the sake of his human visitors had seen better days. So had the moth-eaten curtains masking the windows. There wasn't even a proper phone line, let alone an internet connection, and central heating was a distant prospect. As a half Reaper, I wasn't immune to the freezing temperature, and I huddled inside my coat as I sat down on one of the uncomfortable chairs.

Dad didn't even bother to sit, instead looming over my chair with his arms folded over his chest. "I take it you came here for a reason?"

"I want to know how Mina deflected my Reaper powers," I said without preamble. "I want information. Preferably *before* Halloween."

Dad had seen enough of Mina's capabilities to have an incentive to help us, but he also possessed a Reaper's instinct for secrecy at all costs.

"There's nothing I can give you" was his entirely predictable reply.

"I tried looking everywhere, including the biggest known magical library in the country," I told him. "I asked other Reapers, but you're the one who's plugged into the Council. Far more than old Harold is."

"Am I?"

I threw up my hands. "Stop turning my questions back on me. I know you know who the Founders are, and I have reason to believe Mina might have worked with them to obtain something that helped her deflect my Reaper powers."

"Oh?" His face didn't so much as twitch. "Who told you that?"

"*You* did when you implied the Founders helped her get hold of that book." I hadn't known the Founders were vampires at the time, but Dad had taken the book back to the Reaper Council himself. You'd think he'd have asked a question or two. "It stands to reason that they'd be happy to help someone who wants to break the Reaper Council's rules."

"And has Mina shown any previous connection to the vampires?"

"Well, there was that one vampire who tried to kill me," I said. "You might recall that incident."

"A rogue who is now dead and showed no links to the Founders when I researched his background."

*So he did research the guy.* I'd been starting to think Dad had acquired a convenient case of amnesia since I'd last seen him. "I doubt she gained the ability to repel a scythe by drinking a potion. Have you told the Reaper Council that?"

His scowl deepened. "Obviously, they're aware of her threats to act on Samhain, but I haven't discussed the subject in depth. I rather thought you would prefer for me not to expose your little community to the Council."

Oh crap. He had a point there. Hawkwood Hollow and its ghosts weren't exactly an approved entity. It was more Harold's fault than mine—the local Reaper had hung up his scythe after the floods—but the Reaper Council were merciless. They'd swoop straight in to exorcise the spirits who just wanted to exist peacefully. Never mind that Mina was the more pertinent threat.

"Didn't you at least tell them about the floods twenty years ago?"

"I'm not a witness," he replied. "That's on *your* Reaper to report, and he seems to have no intention of doing so."

"That's because Harold knows better than to trust them to improve the situation." Why had I thought he'd be willing to help, again? "Mina, though… it's barely a week until Halloween."

"Yes, and the Council will already be on the lookout for trouble. Samhain is a common night for people to try making trouble involving the dead."

"I guess," I relented, "but we still need to find out how she deflected my Reaper powers. A rogue coven leader is dangerous enough on her own, but you must have *some* idea how she gained such an ability."

Dad was silent for a long moment. "I believe," he said grudgingly, "that Mina Devlin might have obtained something that belonged to another Reaper. Only a Reaper can fight another Reaper, so it's the logical conclusion."

"How did she obtain this hypothetical object?" I asked. "Either she stole it, or someone gave it to her."

"None of the Council members would betray their oaths."

"Then she stole it," I replied. "Or someone else did. Like a certain group of vampires."

"Vampires," he said, "are *not* the responsibility of the Council. And her one known ally is dead."

"Deader than dead, I know." Frustrated, I rose to my feet and paced the room. "Look—I don't know much about the Founders either, but if no Reaper can lay a hand on Mina, even the Council might have trouble putting her down."

"That's right." Mart popped out of the floor in a manner that would have made any ordinary person jump, but Dad merely gave another sigh. "Don't look so happy to see me."

"How's Mum?" I asked my brother warily.

"She's fine. I distracted her."

His flippant tone instantly set me on edge. "Mart, what did you do?"

"I may have given her your phone number."

I groaned. "Seriously?"

Dad cleared his throat. "You should keep in touch with her. She was devastated the last time you left."

"She doesn't need to get dragged into my fight with Mina," I said. "And you know she's convinced I'm going to be coven leader."

Dad remained unmoved. "Far be it from me to interfere in the coven's business, but the lack of a successor is always going to be a sticking point with your mother."

"And this is my problem... why?" I narrowed my eyes. "Did you forget I was on the road to becoming a fully qualified Reaper before—"

"Before I bit the dust." Mart made exaggerated strangled noises that did not help my mood in the slightest.

"She's completely lost touch with reality." I stalked towards the door. "So have you if you think I'll entertain the notion of moving back here. I like Hawkwood Hollow. It's my home."

"Your home rests on the existence of a group of illegal ghosts."

Oh no. He did not want to start that argument now.

I whipped around. "My home is under threat from a rogue coven leader who's running circles around *your* supervisors. Look there if you want to see a real problem."

I made for the exit, half hoping he'd call me back. But he didn't, and when I opened the door and walked out, only Mart followed me. I shivered a little, but even the freezing October wind was less icy than being inside a Reaper's house.

"I lied," Mart announced. "Mum's not fine. Our other relatives started badgering her after Aunt Rosie managed to escape her office."

"No." My heart plummeted. "Did they see you?"

"They might've got a glimpse before I dived out the window."

Wonderful. I reached up my sleeve and fumbled for my wand, casting a transportation spell without stopping to think. My feet touched down on the hillside near Hawkwood Hollow, and I released a breath. *That was a close one.*

Mart appeared a moment later. "You left me behind!"

"I panicked. Do *you* want to see our relatives?" I *hoped* none of them had followed us home. "I thought not. What else did you lie about? Please tell me you didn't really give Mum my number."

"Okay, I won't tell you."

"Mart." I came to a dead stop—pun intended—when a sudden rush of cold air passed over my skin that had nothing to do with the icy outdoor temperature. "Crap."

"What?" said Mart. "What's crap? Not me, I hope."

I spun on my heel. "Someone just died, Mart."

"I know. Happens all the time."

"That's not what I meant." I scanned our surroundings, but nobody was out walking in the hills in this weather. Not even axe murderers. "I *felt* someone die. A moment ago."

"So?" he said. "Not every death has meaning. Maybe someone fell in a pond."

I might have reprimanded him for his inappropriate jokes if I hadn't guessed he was trying to distract from his own emotions concerning our visit to Greenwood Lake.

Regardless, my paranoia about the timing of the death refused to abate. As we descended the hillside towards Hawkwood Hollow, I tapped into the afterworld. Darkness clouded my vision, but I didn't see any obvious discrepancies.

"Don't do that while we're walking," Mart complained. "It's making my head spin."

"You're *in* the afterworld," I pointed out. "Can you have a look around?"

"Why would I do that?"

"Peace of mind," I said. "Just tell me if you notice any new ghosts. You do that all the time anyway."

He muttered something rude under his breath. "New

ghosts are coming here for Halloween, remember? A whole group of them arrived yesterday."

As if I could forget. "Look, it's easy for you to search the whole town through the afterworld in a minute flat."

"Maybe I had other plans."

"Mart."

He sighed again. "Fine, fine. You owe me a milkshake."

He vanished before I could ask how he possibly expected to drink a milkshake as a ghost, and I walked the rest of the way back to the inn alone.

The restaurant was bustling but not overcrowded. I crossed the room, passing the new ghostly contingent that had arrived yesterday, and found Jia making some kind of sugary dessert in the shape of a ghost for a gap-toothed little girl dressed in pink.

"What's that?" I asked. "New addition to the menu?"

"A trial run," she replied, dubiously surveying her new creation. "I think I overdid it on the sugar."

"It's probably strong enough for even Mart to taste it." I lowered my voice when she handed the sugary abomination over to the small child. "I don't envy her parents having to keep up with her bouncing off the walls for the rest of the afternoon."

"Where *is* Mart?" Jia wiped down the counter. "You're back early. Was the family visit as heinous as you expected?"

"Almost." I spied Allie in the reception area, who gave me a wave from the other side of the connecting door. "Mart's... here."

"Yes, I am." Mart popped up out of the floor and sent a rude gesture towards the group of new ghosts. "Hey! That guy stole my ghost costume."

"We have a half dozen identical costumes," I pointed out. "Did you search the whole town?"

"For what?" Jia smiled at a group of oncoming customers.

"Anything suspicious," I replied vaguely. I waited for her to show the newcomers to an empty table before I continued. "The visit was a washout. Dad said he didn't even speak to the Reaper Council about Mina because he wanted to avoid them showing up here. All he would admit is that Mina might have stolen something from the Reapers that she used to block my powers, but he refused to give specifics."

"If you ask me, that means he doesn't know what they stole," Mart said. "He doesn't like admitting when he doesn't know something either."

"True, but if they have an object in storage that allows one Reaper to repel another's abilities, it's hard to imagine he *doesn't* know it exists."

"Doesn't mean he'll tell us."

"That's also a possibility." I'd have to ask Harold and see if he was any more willing to speak to me. Retired or not, Harold didn't want Mina Devlin to unleash Armageddon any more than the rest of us did.

"The good news is that nobody's dead," Mart said, drifting behind the counter.

Jia raised a brow. "Was there any doubt of that?"

"I… may have sensed something in the afterworld on my way back." I didn't want to start an unnecessary panic, so I added, "Like Mart said, nothing's amiss. I've been a little on edge. I gather nothing dramatic happened while I was gone?"

"Nope." She went over to the new customers to take their orders and returned to the counter. "Oh… a few more ghosts turned up in one of the guest's rooms."

"Seriously?" I groaned. "If they disrupt the tour with unnecessary hauntings, we'll have to kick them out."

"I think they want to act as spectators, not participants."

"I should hope so." Haunting the guests' rooms was bad enough, though there wasn't a single person here who hadn't opted in to get the full Halloween experience. "I hope they aren't expecting us to pay them for contributing."

"Ah... one of them asked for a milkshake in exchange."

"That's what gave you the idea?" I shot my brother an accusing stare, which he ignored.

"You *do* owe me a milkshake." He pointed to a tray of bloodred milkshakes labelled "vampire blood" on a nearby table.

"I'll make one."

As Jia went to oblige, my phone buzzed with a message from Drew asking if I wanted to meet up for a date night at the inn. He wouldn't be asking about date night if someone was dead, so I figured that whatever I sensed had been outside of the town's borders. Yet a nagging doubt remained in the back of my mind.

My Reaper senses couldn't be mistaken. I knew that much.

"Maura!" Allie came into the restaurant, interrupting my train of thought. "I thought you took the morning off."

"I came back early." I'd told her enough about my contentious relationship with my parents for her to know not to pry further. "I can help out here for the rest of the day. I don't mind."

"You were only gone a few hours," said Allie. "We'll be slammed next week. Take all the time off you need while you can."

"She's right." Jia presented Mart with a bloodred milkshake. "There you are. Drink up."

"Don't encourage him," I said out of the corner of my mouth.

Allie raised an eyebrow but otherwise didn't comment; she was used to our weird one-sided interactions with the local ghosts. "Ah... Maura, did you talk to your dad?"

"Yeah. He's as grumpy as ever," I said evasively, knowing

what she really wanted to ask. While Allie was aware of Mina's threats to make a play for power on Halloween, I'd tried to refrain from talking too much about it for Carey's sake.

While Jia moved to stop Mart from knocking the milkshake onto the floor, Allie edged closer to me and whispered, "Did he mention... *her?* Mina?"

I shook my head, guilt squeezing my chest. "Nobody knows where she is."

"Right." Allie gave a quiet sigh. "I really don't want to ruin this for Carey, Maura. Is there anything we can do to prevent her from coming back?"

"We've already put sage outside the inn, but any more than that will repel the ghosts." Not that they seemed to be deterred by our defences.

Allie nodded. "I'm sure the police are trying their best to find her."

"Yeah. Drew's dropping by later, so I'll see what he has to say." I forced a cheery tone. "Really, how many places can an egomaniacal witch with a god complex hide in the north of England?"

That was kind of a rhetorical question because she'd done a spectacular job of evading capture the past few months. And while I didn't know *what* Mina planned to do, she wasn't the sort to make empty threats. It was just my luck that the veil between the living and the dead was thinnest on the same night of the year on which our whole business hinged.

Allie gave another nod. "I hope you're right."

*Me too.*

---

I helped Jia out in the restaurant until Carey came back from school, at which point I went into Halloween-planning mode until Drew showed up for our date.

When three ghosts followed him inside, Carey's familiar, Casper, came running to hide behind my legs.

"Whoa." I caught Drew's arm for balance, and he pulled me into a kiss.

Mart made rude noises behind me, which I ignored.

"Hey." Drew released me and claimed a seat at a table near the window, which was adorned with decorative spiderwebs. "How was the visit? Not as dire as you implied, I assume."

"Yes." I let Casper hide under my seat and glowered at the three transparent newcomers. "Sorry, Drew. Three more ghosts followed you in."

He arched a brow. "Should I be worried about them?"

"No." I rested my chin on my hand. "No, I'm the one who'll have to chase them out of the guests' rooms. Looks like we're the most popular establishment in the afterworld."

"Not the worst time of year for it." He waved across the room at Jia, who'd already started on our drinks. We spent enough time in here for her and the others to know our regular orders without needing to ask. "So... how was it?"

I slumped in my seat. "My mother has my phone number, so I'll never have another peaceful moment again in my life."

"Really?" He blinked. "Isn't she busy as a coven leader?"

"You'd think." I'd already had to turn my phone on silent to stop its constant pinging from distracting me while I was carrying heavy trays of drinks across the room. "She's always been overly emotional, but it's been worse since Mart died. She's set on controlling the life of her living child."

"That's why you left?" he guessed. "It's fine if you don't want to talk about it."

"No... it helps." I was used to burying those unpleasant memories, but you'd think a Reaper would know that things didn't always *stay* buried. In fact, sometimes, the harder I tried to push the memories down, the more likely it was that they'd claw their way out of the ground. "I wanted to see Dad, but someone from the coven would have spotted me and told Mum if I hadn't dropped in to see her too."

"Tricky." He sat back as our food and drinks appeared on the table. "I'm impressed with how quick service is here, considering you must be run off your feet."

"A great time for my mother to start sending me hysterical messages every hour." I picked up my fork. "I know it sounds harsh, but she wanted me to take over from her as coven leader, and she seems to have forgotten the coven kicked me out when I left town. If I'd stayed a minute longer, she'd have signed me up for volunteering at the local academy."

He grinned. "You, volunteering to work with small children?"

"Don't even." She also wanted to meet Drew, which was a horror too deep to contemplate. "Mart distracted her so I could see Dad, but it was a complete waste of time. Dad claimed he can't speak to the Reaper Council without giving away our habit of inviting ghosts to stay in the land of the living."

"Won't the Reaper Council be able to help deal with Mina?" he asked. "He doesn't have to mention Hawkwood Hollow."

"I also wanted to know how Mina gained the ability to deflect my Reaper powers," I said. "He implied that the only way for her to do that is with the help of something she took *from* the Reapers, but he wasn't clear on what that was. Mart suggested he didn't know."

"Might be true," he said. "Your father doesn't seem the sort to admit when he's not in the know."

"You've got that right." The two had met only briefly, but

Dad had made quite the impression on the people he'd encountered during his visit to Hawkwood Hollow. "He wouldn't respond when I mentioned the vampires either."

"Those Founders," he said. "I've asked a few questions at the office, but nobody's heard of them."

"Groups of vampires who illegally procure magical artefacts and rare books are kinda out of the range of the regular police force," I commented. "Dad claimed the vampire he killed wasn't part of their ranks, but I get why he's not keen to bring the Reaper Council any closer to Hawkwood Hollow. "

"Ah." Understanding flickered across his face. "He'll want to give them enough information to stop Mina, but if they ask questions about where she actually came from…"

The trail would lead them straight here. "I know. I don't want them here, either, but Halloween is a week tomorrow, and I don't know that I can stop her on my own."

"You aren't on your own." He reached across the table and took my hand. "We'll find and stop her first."

His confidence warmed me more effectively than a heater, but a cynical voice in my head whispered that it'd been weeks since Jennifer's kidnapping without so much as a peep from Mina. I squeezed Drew's hand back. "So… have you got any new leads?"

"Possibly."

"Wait, you do?" My heart skipped a beat. "Like what?"

"We might have found her location," he replied. "While searching the countryside, my team ran into some kind of spell that turned them around and caused them to get hopelessly lost. They're going back there tomorrow to see if it's a defensive spell designed to keep them away."

"Sounds like one." It didn't mean the hideout belonged to Mina, but how many lone witches with access to powerful misdirection spells might be hiding in the countryside?

"We'll see tomorrow." He returned his attention to his plate. "Otherwise, things are pretty normal."

"Good." Talk of Mina was kind of a mood killer in most situations, let alone on date night, but when another question entered my mind, I blurted it out before I could think better of it. "Has someone died recently?"

"Recently?" he echoed. "When?"

"I sensed a death in the afterworld," I explained. "When I returned to Hawkwood Hollow. I figured that it probably wasn't local, and Mart couldn't find them either."

"Weird," he said. "No deaths have been reported to the police. Are you certain?"

"My Reaper senses are hard to trick."

"Are they, now?" Mart came floating past our table. "Maybe another Reaper will be able to give you a clue."

"What, Harold?" I gave him a warning look when he swiped my fork. "Stop that."

Drew caught my eye. "Your brother? Or one of the other ghosts?"

"My brother." I snatched the fork back. "I think he wants me to ask Harold for his input. Which is barely better than asking my dad."

"Maybe Dad would rather talk to someone with authority." Mart waggled his eyebrows.

I tutted. "I doubt it."

"What?" Drew asked, eyeing the spot where Mart was floating. "Is he talking to me?"

"No… ah. He said Dad might be more likely to talk to you than me." Or he might go into stubborn Reaper mode and refuse to say a word. Besides, Mum had already messaged me with several reminders of her open invitation for Drew to come visit, and the notion was almost as unappealing as a sleepover in Harold's cottage.

"Might he?" Drew asked.

"No. Mart, cut that out." I waved my brother away from the table when he tried to drop glitter into my drink. "I have no idea. I don't know what he's thinking, to be honest."

"If we want to find Mina before Halloween, we might need to pull out all the stops."

*Right.* I dropped my gaze, conscious that my phone had only stopped buzzing with Mum's never-ending text messages because I'd left it in my room before Drew had shown up.

"Maura?" Drew peered at me across the table. "What're you thinking?"

I opened my mouth and found myself asking, "Do you want to meet my parents?"

"Sure." Drew blinked in surprise. "I assume you didn't mean that to sound like a death sentence?"

"Maybe." What had I been thinking? "You've already met my dad."

"Yes, and I survived the experience," he said mildly. "It won't be that bad, will it?"

"Don't speak too soon," I warned. "My mother is… a lot. She'll probably cry on you."

I looked to my brother for confirmation and saw he'd drifted across the room towards the ghost who'd swiped his costume.

"I think I'll survive," Drew answered. "You forget how much of the time I've spent with you has involved dangerous old buildings and dead bodies."

"I'd rather deal with a zombie infestation, to be honest."

Maybe I was being unreasonable. It was Drew's choice whether to come visit or not, and for all I knew, Mum would mellow a little after she spoke to someone who was a living example of the reasons I wanted to stay in Hawkwood Hollow and not return to my old home.

Besides, if we all perished next week, I wouldn't have to go through with the visit after all.

The sound of raised voices cut through my decidedly morose thoughts. Mart, it seemed, had chosen this moment to confront the spirit who was wearing his inflatable ghost costume, and the ensuing ghostly punch-up momentarily banished my trepidation towards the inevitable moment in which Drew and my mother would be in the same room.

*What have I got myself into?*

## 3

The following day dawned with cold and rain, which was pretty standard for October. Drew added to the dismal mood by saying he'd ask around at work and see if anyone had died recently. I offered to drop in later in the day for an update on whether his team had managed to find the source of the misdirection spell that Mina might be using to hide in plain sight.

"I hope it is her," Jia remarked as we started our morning shift. "She's eluded our attention for way too long."

"Yeah." I tipped pumpkin-shaped glitter out of a glass—the stuff got everywhere—and tried to ignore the new group of ghosts clustered in the corner. "She won't have made it easy for the police to find her hideout."

"No, but she's not likely to have left the region." Jia eyed me. "This mysterious death you sensed… might it have been her work?"

"I don't know," I replied honestly. "Drew said he'd look into it, but my Reaper skills don't distinguish between normal deaths and ones that… aren't."

"The timing seems suspicious."

"I thought so, too, but Mart searched the afterworld and didn't find anything weird."

"Oh, I didn't look that hard." Mart came floating past with a lampshade on his head. "The dead person's ghost wouldn't have shown up this soon after their death, would it?"

"I guess not. What's with the lampshade?"

"I'm trying out a new costume."

I raised an eyebrow. "Doesn't have anything to do with losing your fight with that ghost over your last costume, does it?"

Mart stuck his tongue out at me. "No, this one is better."

I shielded my eyes as several bright lights pierced my vision. Mart had hung a string of Christmas lights underneath the lampshade, which glittered when he spun around on the spot.

"Didn't they have Halloween-themed lights?" I swiftly closed my eyes when he attempted to dazzle me again.

When the first customers of the day showed up at the door, I tried once again to put all thoughts of mysterious deaths out of my mind. I didn't quite succeed, but luckily, the day was pretty quiet. The calm before the Halloween storm. While we did have a ghost tour scheduled for that evening, it'd be a lower-key version of the one scheduled to take place in a week, and most guests had saved their bookings for the big night.

During a long stretch of time without any customers, I decided to visit Drew and see if the police had managed to get any more details from his team about Mina's hideout. Oh, and if he'd learned of anything that might point to the strange timing of the death I'd felt. Failing that, I'd ask old Harold. *He* must have noticed. Nothing in the afterworld escaped a Reaper, even a retired old grouch like him.

Mart declined to come with me, claiming he wanted to fine-tune his lampshade costume a little more, so I walked across the bridge over the river by myself. The police station stood on the main high street, an unassuming brick building with transparent automatic doors that opened at my approach.

Typically, a certain blond officer was the one who greeted me on the other side. "What are you doing here?"

I scowled back at Petra. "I thought you were on leave." I did not add *after nearly getting killed by a werewolf*, but from the way her eyes narrowed at me, she'd caught the general gist of my thoughts anyway.

"We don't need your help here, Reaper," she told me.

Evidently, even a brush with death hadn't improved her personality. "Drew told me to come here for an update on his team's hunt for Jennifer."

I'd hoped mentioning the name of the kidnapped coven leader would remind her that there was more at stake than her petty grudge against me. Petra had never been pleased at the notion of a Reaper interfering in police business, and while I'd been responsible for bringing down the vampire that had nearly taken her life, that incident didn't seem to have improved her low opinion of me.

"Maura?" Drew walked out of his office and into the lobby. "Let her in, Petra. I told her to come here."

I plastered on a fake smile as I sidestepped Petra and followed him into his small office. "Did a ghost pee in her coffee this morning?"

"Oh, I told her to stop anyone from getting in who wasn't on the team." He closed the door behind us. "I should have guessed she'd interpret that to mean I wanted *you* to stay out too."

"She was already looking for an excuse to shut me out of the police's business." I didn't bother lowering my voice; it served her right if she was listening on the other side of the door. "Why'd you ask her to keep anyone else from getting in?"

"Secrecy," he replied. "The last thing we need is for one of Mina's people to find out we're potentially on the brink of figuring out her location."

"You really know where she is?" A wary sense of hope underlaid my voice. "You said your team was going back to check that place you found covered in potential misdirection spells..."

"They're still out there," he said. "Coordinating. The problem is that if they draw too much attention to themselves, whoever is hidden behind those spells will either get up and run or attack them outright, and given what we know Mina is capable of..."

"Yeah, best to tread carefully," I finished. "Has she actually been sighted?"

"No, but they've spotted several figures walking in and out of the area covered by the spells," he replied. "They've been using concealment charms, which means they're almost certainly witches. We haven't caught one yet, but it's got to be her followers."

"That or someone who really doesn't want visitors." Most witches were tied to a particular town or village and didn't set up shop in the middle of nowhere. "Have you told Wendy or anyone else in the coven?"

"That didn't seem wise."

I tilted my head to one side. "You think Mina has spies amongst the other witches?"

"It's more likely than I'd prefer."

*True.* Unfortunately. Anyone who'd been in the coven since before Mina's departure was a potential suspect, and even Jennifer's staunch supporters had made zero effort to rescue her from Mina's clutches. They'd claimed Mina would be impossible to find, but I figured the true answer was that they knew they couldn't beat her in combat. Which was fair. *I* wasn't sure I could either, and the notion of our clash being a day or two away made a measure of dread rise to temper the relief I'd momentarily felt at us being close to discovering her location.

I returned to the second unwelcome subject of the day. "How about the death I sensed yesterday. Any news?"

"Nothing." He shook his head. "There weren't any deaths in Hawkwood Hollow, and no news came out of the nearby towns either. That's not to say nobody died at all, but there weren't any calls to the police departments to report anything suspicious."

"All right." I'd put that out of my mind for now. It wasn't worth expending energy on hypotheticals when I had an upcoming clash with my mortal enemy on my hands. "How do you think we should deal with Mina's hideout? Try to get around her defences subtly or blow the whole thing up?"

"That's the problem," Drew said. "Our priorities are to get Jennifer out of there if she's still alive and to take Mina into custody. The former seems more doable than the latter, but they both require a subtle approach that might backfire in our faces if she sees us coming."

"Subtle," I repeated. "That's where it'd be handy to be able to use my Reaper skills to find her."

I'd *tried* to find her—and Jennifer too—through the afterworld, but I'd met nothing but emptiness on the other side. She'd either made herself untraceable or Reaper-proofed her hideout, neither of which boded well for our odds of taking her out.

Rescuing Jennifer, though... *might* be doable. As much as I wanted to make Mina pay for her crimes, the witches seemed incapable of organising themselves without a leader.

If it wasn't already too late for her.

"Harold too," Drew added. "I asked him to join the team. He declined."

"You asked him?" I fought a laugh at the mental image of the old Reaper's face after being asked to help the police. "Shelton might have said yes."

"I haven't seen him since he last showed up in town," said Drew. "Do you think it would help to have another Reaper?"

"By 'another,' I assume that means I'm invited?" I spoke lightly, but there was no way I was sitting this one out. "Can't hurt. I have no idea where Shelton is at the moment, though, and my dad…"

I didn't need to elaborate. Drew knew all about the argument we'd had the previous day.

"Of course you're invited," he said. "Just… don't take unnecessary risks."

"Forgot who you're talking to?" Despite my flippant tone, there was a real danger that anyone who walked into Mina's hideout wouldn't come out again. Reaper or otherwise. "I know the place will be booby-trapped at all angles underneath all those misdirection spells."

"That's why we need to approach carefully," he said. "I've discussed strategies with the team, and we've decided our best bet would be to split up into several groups. Some to engage Mina's attention, others to rescue her hostage."

"If she's there," I added. "She might have more than one hideout. And… well. She might have killed her hostage long ago."

His expression shadowed. "I know."

"When…?" I paused. "When did you plan to go in?"

"As soon as the reports come in." The phone on his desk started ringing. "That'll be my team. I'll let you know when we're ready, okay?"

"All right." My heart gave an uneven jolt. *Today*. With a

week to go before Halloween, we couldn't afford to waste any more time.

I left the police station and nearly collided with a tall, shadowy figure holding a scythe. I sprang backward into the doorway then relaxed when I recognised the figure's scowling face beneath a hood that I'd never seen him wear before. "Oh, it's you, Harold."

What was old Harold doing out of his cottage? And why was he dressed as a full Reaper, even carrying his scythe?

"You're remarkably unobservant for a Reaper," he said by way of a greeting.

"Are you going to the police station?" I decided to let the insult slide. "Changed your mind about joining Drew's team?"

"Didn't you sense it?" he asked cryptically.

"Sense what?" I blinked at him in confusion. "I didn't sense anything today. Yesterday, though…"

"A Reaper,'" he said, "was killed yesterday."

"A *Reaper?*" My jaw hung open, questions exploding in my mind. "Who? Where?"

I looked wildly around, as though a dead Reaper would be lying in Hawkwood Hollow's high street. Which was ridiculous, but seeing old Harold walking around was as odd a sight as a ghoul in daylight.

"Stop drawing attention to yourself," he growled.

"Says the man with the scythe." I glared at him. "Seriously. What Reaper? How do you even know?"

"When a Reaper dies, it's not the same as a regular death," he said. "No traces are left behind, and nobody but other Reapers can sense their demise. I suppose your senses aren't attuned enough to be able to tell the difference."

"Thanks," I said. "I was out of town at the time and only sensed someone die when I landed outside Hawkwood Hollow. Who *was* it?"

"I wouldn't know."

How did he manage to project such a menacing air and yet be utterly unhelpful? "Then what's with the dramatics?"

"A death of *any* Reaper is a cause for concern."

"It wasn't Shelton, was it?" I asked warily.

"I haven't checked."

"I thought you were friends." Though the word might have been too strong to use in the context of the grumpy resident Reaper. "Why are you at the police station?"

"The Reaper Council has yet to deign to answer my calls," he said. "I thought I'd see if the police had better luck."

"Well, they might have found Mina's hideout." I lowered my voice, conscious that Drew hadn't wanted word to spread outside the station. "Don't tell anyone else. Drew could use your help, though, if you've changed your mind about joining the team...?"

Instead of answering, he entered the police station and marched straight past a startled Petra. *I'll take that as a no.*

What if Shelton *had* been the Reaper whose death we'd sensed? Harold wouldn't have been that flippant if that was the case, surely, but if no body or soul had been left behind, there'd be no way to identify the victim.

More to the point, a Reaper's death could only be the work of one person.

*Mina.*

I paced down the high street and ducked into an alley away from any onlookers. Then I called upon the afterworld, peering into the darkness that streamed from my hands at my command. *Shelton?*

Each person had a signature of sorts, and Reapers burned brighter than most. I held an image of Shelton in my mind and stepped into the dark.

My feet sank into mud. I slipped and staggered, catching

my balance against a figure who was tall, shadowy, and very much alive.

"You!" said Shelton, stepping away from me. "What the devil are you doing?"

"I sensed a Reaper die," I said. "So did Harold. Thought I'd make sure it wasn't you."

"Clearly, it wasn't." He faced me, his own scythe strapped to his back. "Were you worried?"

"Yes, believe it or not," I said. "Reapers who are actually on my side are hard to come by. What're you doing out here in the middle of nowhere?"

"Assisting your police."

I startled, my gaze panning over the muddy field. "Is this where... where the police are hunting Mina?"

"Assuming she didn't see you jump out of thin air, yes."

"How was I supposed to know?" I called the afterworld again, cloaking myself in darkness and hoping Mina wasn't looking out the window at that precise moment. "Harold didn't say you were helping the police. I just ran into him outside the station, and he claimed he didn't know which Reaper was killed either."

"The Council will know," he growled. "It's not worth concerning ourselves with."

"Not even if Mina was responsible, I guess." A shiver ran down my spine. "I can ask my dad, but he's trying to avoid the Council at the moment."

He'd have certainly sensed the Reaper's death regardless, but would that have driven him to risk getting in touch with them? Maybe I hadn't given him enough credit for his willingness to avoid drawing attention to Hawkwood Hollow for my sake.

"Spoken to him recently, have you?" Shelton queried.

"Yesterday." I scanned the fields on either side of us, but no signs of any hidden buildings leapt out at me. Which was the point, I supposed. "Erm... *how* close to Mina's place are we?"

"Not enough to get caught in the misdirection spell." Shelton pointed diagonally across the fields. "We think it's somewhere over there, but we'll have to act soon, before Mina realises that we're onto her."

"Drew's talking to the rest of the team on the phone." I followed his gaze. "I don't see them."

"They went to reconvene. I didn't see the need to join them."

"Being antisocial, are you?" I guessed. "Dad told me that Mina might have stolen something from the Reaper Council. To block our powers, I mean. Or her vampire allies did the thieving for her."

"Did he, now?" He tilted his head. "Did he say more?"

"No... I'm not sure he knew *what* she stole, but it's an explanation for how she managed to Reaper-proof herself." I gave the fields another surreptitious glance. "I guess she did the same to her hideout too. Drew wants to get Jennifer out first, but we're at a disadvantage."

Especially if she'd killed a Reaper. The questions were how and why.

*Dammit. Dad's the person to ask.* I couldn't talk to the Council myself, and if a Reaper had really died... it was safe to say their eyes would turn in this direction sooner rather than later.

It looked as though I might have to take my boyfriend to meet my parents a tad sooner than I'd planned.

# 4

Shelton had nothing more to share with me, so I left him in the field and returned to the inn. Before I entered the lobby, I called Dad's number.

"Hey," I said when he picked up. "I have a question. Did a Reaper—?"

"Don't ask me questions on the phone," he snapped. "It's too easy for our calls to be intercepted."

"I didn't know you were that tech savvy," I remarked. "What, do you think Mina tapped your phone line?"

"Witches are adept at spying," he said. "I told you I'd get in touch if I had news. And I don't."

*He didn't forget our argument, I take it.*

"Didn't you sense...?" I scrambled for a vague way of phrasing the question. "Something related to, erm, Reapers? Yesterday?"

"I told you," he said, "I won't say a word on the phone."

"Will you tell me in person?" I pushed on. "Listen, we're going after Mina... ah, soon. If you can help us avoid getting killed in there, I'd really appreciate the help."

"I'll tell you *if* you refrain from taking any reckless actions today."

"Today." He'd read between the lines of my words. "Would you be inclined to speak to Drew if I brought him with me?"

His faint sigh reached me through the phone. "Yes, but you know who else will want to speak to him."

*Mum definitely will.* "I'll risk it. I'll let you know when we're coming."

I messaged Drew, asking if his team would consider delaying their infiltration of Mina's hideout for another day. He replied that Harold had just asked the exact same question, and the team was still arguing about the logistics of storming Mina's base when nobody had managed to find their way around the misdirection spells yet.

Unlike Dad, Drew didn't mind sharing the details over the phone, and while his team would be less than enthused at the idea of their head officer leaving town at a time like this, he told me he could spare an hour tomorrow morning before they made a move on Mina's hideout.

I was about to call Dad and tell him the same when my phone began buzzing with another call. Mum. *Oh no.*

"Maura!" she said. "You never said you were coming back to visit again so soon."

She had to be kidding me. "Did *you* intercept Dad's phone line?"

"Is it so wrong that I want to know what you're up to?" She spoke with a sob in her voice. "You haven't been answering my messages."

"I literally saw you yesterday," I pointed out. "I haven't had time to do anything worth telling you about. It's just work stuff."

"I always want to hear about your life!" she insisted. "Tell me everything."

"I can't talk now," I told her. "I'll drop by tomorrow morning after I see Dad."

"You'll bring your boyfriend, right?" she pressed. "I'll have to clean the house to be ready for both of you."

"That's unnecessary," I said. "We won't be able to stay long anyway. I'll let him know, and I'll see you soon."

I should have guessed that I wouldn't be able to see Dad without her wanting a piece of me, too, but I hadn't thought she'd go as far as to eavesdrop on my phone calls. If she'd been anyone other than my mother, I'd have responded by cutting her out of my life, but it'd be impossible to walk away again as long as I had to keep dragging myself to Dad's house to convince him to help us take on Mina.

Regardless of how much Mum's behaviour annoyed me, I would rather she didn't know about the situation with Mina. She didn't need that burden on her shoulders on top of running a coven and mourning a dead child who wasn't quite gone.

Hmm. Maybe Mart could be convinced to distract her again.

---

"Oh no," Mart said. "Not a chance. Why are you springing this on me now?"

*Because I knew you'd say no.* I wasn't proud of it, but I'd waited until the morning instead of asking him the previous day, and we were already waiting for Drew in the lobby of the inn when I asked Mart if he wouldn't mind distracting Mum and the rest of the family while Drew and I talked strategy with Dad.

"You usually *like* causing trouble," I said.

"I don't." He folded his arms. "Have your detective distract her instead."

"We're supposed to be speaking to Dad," I said. "If Mum monopolises our attention all day, we'll have zero chance of getting anywhere with convincing him to help us stop Mina."

"Then go to see Dad first."

"That's the plan, but Mum's been texting me all night thanks to a certain someone giving her my phone number." Which hadn't in any way improved my mood that morning. "You owe me for that."

"And you owe me for letting that ghost steal my costume."

"There are a dozen identical costumes in storage." I rubbed my forehead, feeling a headache brewing. "Unless you want me to tell Mum that we're being threatened by an evil megalomaniac witch who wants us dead?"

"I'm already dead."

Luckily, Drew chose that moment to walk in through the automatic doors and wrap me in a hug. "Ready?" he asked.

"Not really." I reluctantly let go of him. "Have your team seen any movement near Mina's hideout?"

"Not yet, but they're getting impatient," he said. "The longer we wait, the more likely it is that Mina will move elsewhere or otherwise strike first. We'll need to act today, one way or another."

My mouth went dry. "Yeah. I know. I'll try to convince Dad to come with us."

Given his attitude on the phone the previous day, the odds were decidedly stacked against me, but I had to try.

It would have been easier if Mum would have stopped texting me for longer than five minutes. My phone was on silent, but it kept on buzzing in my pocket as we left the inn. I'd given Drew the news that she expected him to stop by, and he'd reiterated that he didn't mind despite my dire warnings. At least if Mart didn't come with us, there might be less chance of the waterworks. Or not.

I opted to shortcut the journey by using a transportation

spell on both of us. Drew and I vanished and then reappeared in front of the grand house in which the Reaper lived. The door opened before I could knock, and Shelton came walking out of my dad's house.

"What are you doing here?" I took a startled step back.

"Just dropping by." His gaze slid over to Drew. "Possibly for the same reasons as you."

"Wait—" I broke off when he vanished into the afterworld, leaving a Shelton-shaped shadow behind him. "What's with the local Reapers and their unnecessary dramatics?"

The door had begun to close, and I hurried to intercept my dad in the doorway. "We're here. What were you talking to Shelton about?"

"Reaper business." My dad, too, surveyed my companion. "So you did bring Drew with you."

"That's right," I replied. "He has information to share with you."

We followed him into the house, where I perched on the edge of an uncomfortable seat and broached the first unwelcome subject of the day. "I sensed a Reaper die not long after I left here yesterday. I'm guessing you know who it was."

Dad's face barely changed. "Nobody you're familiar with."

That was a non-answer if I ever heard one. "I already talked to Harold and Shelton. Both implied that it was Mina's work."

"You came here to tell me what I already knew?"

"You're the one who refused to have a conversation on the phone." I reeled my temper back in. "We also know where Mina's hideout is. We're going there today to get Jennifer back. Right, Drew?"

He inclined his head. "I understand that the Reaper Council is committed to secrecy, but Mina is a threat to the Reapers and the rest of the paranormal world alike. We would do better to join forces to ensure that she's brought to justice."

"Indeed?" Dad queried. "You might have forgotten that your girlfriend put me in a difficult position by announcing her intention to protect a town of illegally preserved ghosts, and she continues to act outside of the Council's laws."

"You think the Council will show up if you help us?" I pushed to my feet. "If Mina's capable of *killing* one of them, you'd think they'd have already taken notice."

"Yes," he said, "they will certainly have noticed. That's what Shelton and I were discussing. You'll choose to protect the ghosts over involving the Council in bringing Mina to justice, no doubt."

"What?" I gaped at him. "I have zero control over anything the Council does, but the ghosts have nothing to do with our clash with Mina. We're not letting her invade Hawkwood Hollow."

"You speak as though you have a choice in the matter," Dad said. "Mina has her sights set on your town. You know that."

"And we have her hideout in *our* sights." I refused to let his stubborn pessimism bring me down. "Can the Reaper Council even find someone who's made herself Reaper-proof, or would they need us to smoke her out first?"

"Exactly," Drew added. "My team is ready to move in on Mina's hideout regardless of the Reaper Council's opinions on the matter. I'm assuming they aren't willing to discuss their own strategies with other magical authorities?"

The irritation in his tone surprised me, but perhaps it shouldn't have. Drew wasn't supposed to defer to the Reaper Council, and he knew how hard I'd worked to keep the ghosts of Hawkwood Hollow safe.

"They don't even discuss their strategies with the other Reapers." I indicated Dad, who scowled in response. "Dad, you know we're on the same side, and we don't have time to wait for the Reaper Council to realise that. Whether they intend to act against Mina or not doesn't matter. We have the information to find her."

"And how exactly did you plan to counter her ability to prevent any Reaper from harming her?" Dad enquired. "Shelton told me you didn't have a plan, short of taking her by surprise."

"She's hidden her hideout with misdirection spells, which makes it tricky for *anyone* to get near her," I pointed out. "The more of us who join Drew's team, the more likely it is that we'll find a gap in her defences."

"I have a team of a dozen wizards waiting on standby," said Drew. "We have the aid of the Reaper Shelton, too, and I'd like to extend that request to you."

*He's going to say no*, I thought with a sinking heart. "Dad. I know you think you're supposed to be impartial, but it's not like you'd be helping in a random coven war. This is bigger than that."

"It's also for the Council to decide, not me," he said. "Mina has undoubtedly stolen from the Reapers' own possessions as well as murdering one of their own. She'll face their wrath, make no mistake."

"You think she's going to sit patiently and wait for the Reaper Council to show up to arrest her?" I shook my head. "We have six days before Halloween, and since we already know where she's hiding…"

"Do you?" Dad faced Drew. "Whereabouts is this supposed hideout of hers?"

In answer, Drew pulled out his phone and tapped on the screen, pulling up a map of the area.

I figured Dad would find that too technologically advanced to comprehend, but he examined the screen with apparent interest and then tutted. "That is not your witch's hideout."

"Says who?" I frowned. "How could you possibly know that?"

"I know because I've looked around the area myself," he retorted. "There *are* witches hiding there, but they belong to a faction that are working against Mina Devlin. You might know of them."

"What—the ones who came to hunt down the vampire?" Like Priscilla, who'd turned against Mina from the inside at a risk to herself to hunt down her allies... and who, come to think of it, I hadn't seen since she'd nearly died at the vampire's hands. I'd been under the impression she'd still been hospitalised. "That's where they're hiding?"

"Yes," Dad said. "If you'd gone there yourself, you'd have been able to get in."

"It's Reaper-proofed." Who other than Mina would be able to achieve such a feat?

"It isn't," he said. "If you'd used your abilities to track one of those witches, you'd have been able to get straight in."

"Er... does Shelton know that?"

"I enlightened him," he said. "He should know better than to take orders from the police."

"Hey, Drew's the one in charge of law enforcement in Hawkwood Hollow, remember?" I wouldn't stand for him insulting Drew in front of my face. "Don't blame him for not having a Reaper's super-senses."

"If it's true, my team will want proof," Drew added.

"We'll go there ourselves," I decided. "Dad, you'd tell us if you *did* find Mina's actual hideout, wouldn't you?"

"Yes, as I told you yesterday." His voice dropped to a disapproving growl. "Now, if you don't mind, I'm expecting a visit from the Reaper Council, during which I'll have to convince them not to go near Hawkwood Hollow in search of the person who killed one of their members."

"Did they actually tell you they were coming?" It was just like Dad to bury that bombshell at the tail end of our conversation. "Or do they just pop up out of nowhere?"

"The latter, and as the Reaper closest to where one of their own was killed, I'll be their natural choice to question."

"You know who it was, right?"

"Yes." A heartbeat passed. "It was the Reaper to whom I handed that book of Mina's for safekeeping."

*"Dad."* The book of dark magic. Mina had stolen it back.

"Go on." He waved us towards the door, heedless of the fury boiling inside my chest. "Let me handle the Council."

"You can't just *say* that—" I spluttered.

Drew took my shoulder and gently steered me towards the door. I uttered a torrent of curses that got no response from Dad aside from a disapproving shake of the head. Then we were outside, and the door closed at our backs.

"He is *unbelievable*," I snarled. "She stole the book. *Again.*"

"She won't have had time to read it all yet," Drew attempted to reassure me.

"That doesn't matter." I stalked away from the Reaper's house. "We can't even get into her hideout."

Just where *was* Mina hiding if not there?

"Yes… I'll have to call my team," Drew said. "Ah—did you still want to see your mother?"

"I probably don't have a choice." I'd been ignoring my phone's incessant buzzing while we'd been in Dad's house, but she'd never let me leave Greenwood Lake without dropping in to visit. "She's already tapped Dad's phone, and she'll have people watching us. I guarantee it."

"That seems excessive." He followed my path downhill towards the lake. "Why does she need to spy on her own family members?"

"She wants to exert control." I sought to explain Mum's behaviour in a way that didn't sound unhinged, even if it was. "You know, I took off at eighteen, right after Mart died. Not because of what she did, but my extended family booted me out of the coven and generally tried to blame me for his death. Don't worry, we won't be meeting *them*."

Not if I had anything to do with it.

"Where's your brother, anyway?" he asked. "Did he stay behind?"

"Unfortunately." I picked out a boat to take us to the island in the lake's centre. "He refused to let me talk him into distracting the others. Last time, he locked my Aunt Rosie in her office to keep her from bugging us." Drew's look of alarm prompted me to add, "She deserved it. She's wanted my mum to step down since Mart died, which is another reason Mum's so set on me coming back to become her successor."

Understanding flickered across his face. "Coven politics. I can see why you wanted to keep Mina's coven at arm's length when you moved to Hawkwood Hollow."

"And yet here I am."

This time, we'd be visiting Mum at home, a smaller house that lay next to the coven's headquarters and that would give us a little more privacy than if we crammed ourselves into her office.

Drew's expression showed no hints that my revelations had fazed him, but dread gripped me as we approached Mum's house. The red-painted door sprang open the instant my knuckles touched the wooden surface, and Mum emerged with a squeal of joy. "You came! Oh, and you must be Drew."

"It's great to meet you." He tried for a handshake, but Mum drew him into a hug that was way too intense for someone she'd just met. I shot him an apologetic look, but my mother was already steering him into the hallway.

"How long have you known Maura?" She released a breathless stream of questions on the way to the living room, which hadn't changed an inch in the past two decades. Pink lace draped every surface, and the terrible artwork my brother and I had produced at school still adorned the walls. "How long have you been together? Are you—?"

"Mum, that's enough," I interjected. "Let the man breathe."

Drew gave her a smile that was far more convincing than mine as he took a seat in one of the lace-covered armchairs. "It's fine."

Mum beamed right back. "Well, he's polite, I'll say that much. How *did* you meet?"

"We met a few months ago, when Maura came to Hawkwood Hollow," he replied. "We... hit it off right away."

I raised a brow at him. We'd almost hated each other at first, but I didn't blame him for not wanting to get into the details in front of my mother. I hadn't come up with a parent-appropriate cover story, but it was hard to know how Mum would actually respond.

At least her living room had comfortable chairs, unlike Dad's. As I claimed the seat next to Drew's, I spied Mart hovering near a row of family portraits I'd drawn at school.

"There you are," I called to my brother. "I thought you weren't coming."

"Oh, Mart's been wonderful," Mum said distractedly. "Drew, you can see ghosts too?"

"No, he's a werewolf," I replied. "Didn't I tell you that?"

"No, of course you didn't," she said. "A werewolf, really? Interesting choice."

I tensed. "We liked one another. Him being a werewolf didn't factor into it."

I hadn't thought she had anything in particular against werewolves. I mean, she'd had two children with a Reaper, so she could hardly judge me for my own romantic choices, but

I'd forgotten how unpredictable she could be. Though I might have said the same for Mart, who was currently fixing a fake moustache upon my appalling eight-year-old's drawing of our family as stick figures. Dad was represented as a black smudge holding a scythe.

Mum began a new barrage of questions, which Drew answered with far more patience than I possessed on a good day. It was hard to give too many details about Hawkwood Hollow without mentioning how it'd ended up being infested with ghosts, but Drew's inability to see the dead helped somewhat. Until she asked the inevitable question.

"So, is there no coven in Hawkwood Hollow?" she asked. "You didn't mention one."

"No… yes, but they're not important."

"Lucky them." She gave a laugh. "I'm under constant scrutiny here. That dreadful Rosie is always nitpicking—and don't get me started on Great-Aunt Agatha."

"She needs a hobby." The problem with such a small town was that there was only one position as coven leader and too many witches to share the limelight.

"She says I've lost my touch." She laughed again, a brittle sound. "As she's been saying for years. It would *help* if I had a suitable successor, but you…"

*Here we go again.* "I was never in the running. I was a pariah from birth, practically."

Anyone who wasn't in the coven was an outsider. Not that I'd ever had a chance of being anything else, being half-Reaper, and Mum's attempt to recast my history to suit her demands was wearing thin. Especially in front of my boyfriend.

"Oh, don't be silly." She turned to Drew. "I'm glad she finally met someone, even if it isn't *quite* what I expected. Since losing her brother, she lost herself for a while."

"I'm still here," Mart objected.

"It's true," I said, unable to help myself. "He *is* still here. And while he *is* what wrecked my past relationships, it's not because he's dead. It's because he's annoying."

Mart threw a lace-covered cushion at me. Instead of smiling at my attempt to lighten the mood, Mum began crying again. *Oh god.*

"It's been so hard," she said to Drew between sobs. "I thought she'd never settle down. I'm going to miss her."

"Mum," I said through gritted teeth. "I'm not *settling down*, I'm choosing a new place to live, and that doesn't mean I'm never going to visit. I'm here right now."

"And me," Mart said. "Tell you what—*I'll* be your successor."

*Okay, it's time to go.* I climbed to my feet. "We should be going now. Right, Drew?"

Mum sniffed, her eyes watery. "You only just got here!"

"I did tell you Drew was busy," I said. "So am I, but we'll come again another time."

"Right." She sniffed, tears leaking from her eyes. "Don't let me keep you."

*Maybe I do have more important matters to deal with,* I thought caustically. Like the potential apocalypse, for instance.

Not that we were any closer to finding Mina's hideout. While Dad's revelation had reminded me that we had other potential allies in the former coven members, I just wished that it hadn't sent us racing back to square one when it came to taking down Mina.

5

"Sorry about that," Drew said after I'd cast a transportation spell to return us to the road leading into Hawkwood Hollow.

"What do you have to be sorry for?" I shook my head. "If anything, I should apologise for inflicting my mother on you when I knew exactly what she'd be like."

"And *I* knew what I was getting into," he said. "Besides, she's not as bad as some of my own extended family. Pack members, you know."

"At least they don't message you every hour of the day." My phone buzzed *again*. "If I miss anything important because of her…"

"You haven't discussed payment with me yet for distracting her," Mart accused.

"I thought you stayed behind." I winced when my phone's buzzing intensified as though there was a wasp's nest trapped inside. "Also, you gave her my number, remember? If anything, she's been *worse* since we resumed contact."

"Ah—I'll have to talk to my team before we go to find

those witches," Drew said apologetically. "They'll want to hear from me in person."

That figured. "I don't mind going alone."

"It might be dangerous."

"Not if the witches are scheming against Mina too." Which I assumed they were if they'd gone to such lengths to hide themselves. "They're potential allies."

He inclined his head. "Still, be careful. They might not be on Mina's side, but they're crafty enough to fool Shelton into thinking they were her."

"Not on purpose." Shelton had taken the police's word that it was Mina. So had I, for that matter. "Who knows—maybe they know where Mina is *really* hiding."

While Drew began to walk away, Mart cleared his throat loudly. "I have no interest in meeting the witches."

"All right," I said. "See you at the inn."

I pictured the field in which I'd run into Shelton the previous day and stepped into the afterworld.

As my feet touched down in the muddy field, the darkness faded. I then surveyed the area for any signs of a concealment spell, but nothing obvious leapt out at me.

*Let's find those witches.*

Pulling out my wand, I began to walk, engaging my Reaper senses to keep from being led astray. Darkness cloaked my path, forming a tunnel that made it easy to spot the shimmering edges of a misdirection spell.

"You won't get me that easily," I muttered, sidestepping the spell's shimmering curtain.

Straight into a swamp.

My feet skidded in waterlogged mud, and my arms pinwheeled as I frantically sought to keep my balance. *Really smooth, Maura.*

Already second-guessing this misadventure, I shuffled out of the swamp and realised I'd completely lost sight of the shimmering effects of the misdirection spell. I tapped into the afterworld again, and the air began to shimmer with another hidden spell.

I moved closer, glimpsing a figure half-hidden beneath a transparent cloak. "Hey—"

Sparks flew out as a middle-aged woman cloaked in black pointed her wand directly at my face. "You."

"Hey."

Her wand began to spark again.

"Erm. I think there's been a misunderstanding."

As I backed away, more figures popped up on all sides, having presumably been hiding under concealment spells the whole time, and pointed their wands at me.

"Wait." I held up my hands, but given the shadows leaking from my palms, that wasn't exactly a usual gesture of surrender. "I'm not here to start a fight. Didn't Priscilla tell you who I was?"

"We know who you are." The black-clad witch stepped to the head of their group, her rippling cloak making her look as though she was auditioning to be the next Grim Reaper. Minus the scythe, of course. "You're the Reaper Witch."

"Then you'll know I want to find Mina as much as you do." I lowered my hands. "Or I assume that's why you're hiding under a dozen concealment spells in the middle of nowhere."

"We don't need your help." The witch lowered her wand, but the hostility in her expression didn't abate. She was easily twice my age, but she spoke like a petulant teenager.

"That's pleasant." I scanned the group, not recognising any faces beneath their pointed hats. Maybe Priscilla was still recovering from her ordeal at the vampire's hands, but I'd have thought her allies would have *some* desire to hear me out. "I'm also working with the police and three other Reapers. Are you sure you want to spurn all of us?"

"Mina is capable of resisting any Reaper," said the black-cloaked witch. "And you're not enough of a witch to beat her either."

"I never said I could beat her single-handedly. Can you?" I challenged. "For that matter, do you happen to know *how* she made herself immune to Reapers? I have information you might find valuable. We can help one another."

"I highly doubt that," said the witch haughtily. "I was in line to be coven leader until Mina stepped in. You were kicked out of your own coven, weren't you?"

"Have you been spying on me?" I'd have thought they'd save that energy for thwarting Mina rather than undermining their potential allies, but if nothing else, my latest visits to Greenwood Lake had been a screaming reminder of how petty grudges amongst coven members could override common sense. "I chose to leave my coven. Like I did my Reaper apprenticeship. That doesn't mean I have nothing to offer you. Did you know that I helped catch Mina's vampire ally?"

"That's true." Priscilla came striding up to join the others. "Isabella, I think she can help us. She's been talking to the other Reapers. She'll have information we can't access."

*There she is.* I'd wondered if she might show her face again, but I hadn't known her allies had been lurking so close to Hawkwood Hollow. "Exactly."

The black-cloaked witch—Isabella—regarded Priscilla with a frown. "I thought you didn't want the Reapers involved either."

"Yes, why not exclude the one group of people who can stop Mina from doing—whatever she plans to do on Samhain." I back-pedalled, not wanting to share the details until they agreed to reciprocate. "I was there when she admitted she plans to strike on that night, and we have less than a week. If you want to find her before then…"

"We're better off joining forces," Priscilla finished. "Isabella, we can invite her to our next meeting, can't we?"

"What, like a coven meeting?" I gave a head count of the group. Nine witches, which wasn't enough for a full coven. Not enough to fight Mina either. *They do need my help.*

"Yes." Priscilla inclined her head. "I'd say this is urgent enough for her to come to tonight's meeting, right, Isabella?"

"Urgent." Isabella made a sceptical noise. "Mina's on the run, and most of her allies are in prison."

*Except she killed a Reaper. And we don't know how many other allies she has out there.*

"Then why haven't you managed to find her yet?" I propped a hand on my hip. "For that matter, have you spoken to any of the current members of Hawkwood Hollow's coven? They want their leader back. I bet they'd be willing to join forces too."

"Useless fools," Isabella spat. "They let Mina kidnap their leader in broad daylight."

"Also, they might be compromised," Priscilla added. "Nobody formerly associated with Mina can be trusted."

*Speak for yourself,* I thought. She might have had a point, but Isabella's outright hostility made the notion of her agreeing to join forces as unlikely as me going line dancing with Harold the Reaper.

"And yet you want to invite a Reaper to one of our meetings?" said one of the other witches. "What if she can't be trusted either?"

"I suppose you'll just have to take the risk." I rolled my eyes. "I thought I was ineffective, not traitorous. Make up your minds."

"Come to the coven meeting," Priscilla said firmly. "It's at eight tonight. Isabella, we should let her show us what information she has."

*Only if you reciprocate.* I waited for Isabella to argue.

But she gave a reluctant nod. "Fine. Come here tonight. You'll get one shot to prove yourself."

"I will." I watched them turn around and vanish beneath the haze of a concealment spell. Then I turned back to the shadows and stepped into the dark.

I landed outside the inn then checked the time. I'd missed the morning shift for the second day in a row, which wasn't ideal, but I'd be able to help Jia and Allie in the lunchtime rush. The restaurant was buzzing with customers, and I walked through yet another new contingent of ghosts on my way upstairs to change out of my muddy clothes.

When I came downstairs, Allie was busy helping a group of guests check in, which spared me from having to relive the dire experience of taking Drew to meet my mother. In the restaurant, I found Jia expertly making blood-coloured milkshakes while Mart sang "This Is Halloween" from *The Nightmare Before Christmas* in the background.

"You're late," he said, spotting me. "Did you bring me a present?"

"I got us an invitation to a coven meeting, if that counts."

"No, it doesn't." He tried to swipe one of the milkshakes, but Jia pulled it out of his reach. "Spoilsport."

"What coven meeting?" Jia asked between pouring drinks. "I thought you were visiting your parents with Drew."

"I was," I replied. "I figured Mart would have told you I went on an excursion on the way back. It turns out the place we thought Mina was hiding in actually belongs to Priscilla and a bunch of other former coven members."

"Oh." Her expression sharpened with understanding. "I did wonder if they were still in the area. They invited you to a meeting?"

"That sounds like a trap," Mart said. "How do you know they won't capture you as well?"

"They haven't captured anyone." Isabella's attitude left

much to be desired, but I was willing to tolerate a meeting with a group of grumpy witches if it paved the way to stop Mina from enacting her plan. "I don't want to pass up the opportunity to get more allies. Isabella doesn't seem to like me much, but Priscilla almost died fighting the vampire. She convinced the others to hear me out."

"I know her," she said. "Isabella, I mean. She's not likely to be on Mina's side, but she's the traditionalist sort. She can't be thrilled to invite a Reaper to her coven meeting."

"I got that impression too." I waited for Jia to deliver the milkshakes to a nearby table before I continued to speak. "It's a bizarre setup they seem to have going on. Their hideout is concealed under a dozen layers of misdirection spells. Even when I tried to use my Reaper skills to find it, I landed in a swamp."

Mart cackled. "Wish I'd seen that."

"Hilarious," I said. "And yet all they seem to be doing is holding meetings like a regular coven, not tracking Mina."

"It might be that they didn't want to give any of their strategies away in front of a potential enemy," Jia said. "They'll likely go into more detail during the meeting."

"Or lock you in the cellar," Mart said helpfully. "Haven't you had enough coven nonsense for one day?"

"For a lifetime, yes, but this is important." I turned to Jia, exasperated. "You don't think I'm making a mistake by going to meet them?"

"Hard to tell, but it's worth a shot," she replied. "Tell you what—I'll come with you."

"Are you sure?"

She nodded. "It'll keep you from running into trouble."

"That'll be the day," Mart said. "The best outcome is that it'll turn out they've been sitting in their hidey-hole, arguing about the colour of their coven's hats for the past few decades."

"They can't have been hidden there *that* long." No, they'd likely stepped up their security after Mina had gone on the run. "I'm sure they'll have a little information to share that might help us find Mina. Or rule them out as another threat."

"Nah, they aren't a threat," Jia said. "More importantly, how did your parents take to Drew?"

I blinked at the abrupt change of subject, though I ought to have expected it. "My dad already met him, remember? He was the one who gave me the news that we hadn't found Mina's hideout after all."

"Oh." She glanced at Mart. "And your mother...?"

"As unbearable as always." I risked pulling out my phone to see the barrage of messages that had stacked up since I'd left. "What do you do when you want to keep someone in your life but also at arm's length?"

"Tie them to a wall?" Mart suggested.

"I was talking about Mum."

"I know."

Jia cleared her throat. "I don't know. Sorry. If it's any consolation, I don't think you did anything wrong by trying."

"It probably doesn't help that I was tying myself in knots to avoid mentioning Mina." I ducked around Mart to make myself a coffee. I was in dire need of a caffeine fix after the morning I'd had. "It's kinda hard to mention Hawkwood Hollow at all without straying close to the subject."

"Is it?" Jia queried. "Did you tell her about the ghosts?"

"Yes... a little." To clarify, I added, "If I mentioned I'd made friends with a bunch of ghosts, she'd have taken it as more proof of how irreparably damaged I am after losing my twin. She went into absolute hysterics when I mentioned the inn was haunted."

"Also, I'm not lost," Mart said unnecessarily. "And she was fine before you showed up."

"Fine?" I echoed. "You weren't even talking to her. You were sticking fake moustaches on my family portraits."

"You have family portraits?" Jia asked.

"Not real portraits—my crappy art from school," I corrected. "And it's true. Not that I'm ungrateful that you went to distract her, Mart—"

"You *are* ungrateful." He pouted. "And I'm telling the truth as well. We had a lovely chat about the ghost-tour business before you barged in."

"Barged in? I was invited." Honestly. "Wait. You didn't tell her about Mina, did you?"

"I didn't need to." He gave me a withering look. "It's no wonder she's messaging you at all hours if you're refusing to tell her anything at all."

"I told her about Drew!" I said indignantly. "I brought him to meet her."

"Did you mention me?" Jia asked.

"Yes, briefly, but she doesn't let me get a word in edgeways—" My phone went off with yet another buzzing sound. "Not when she's typing either."

Maybe I should have tried harder, though. Mart had a point. I *had* been fixated on avoiding letting anything slip about Mina, to the extent that I'd been sparse with the details of my new life. Telling her more might not stop the deluge of messages, but we had less than a week until Halloween. I might as well offer her a little. Just in case I wasn't around in a week's time.

*Cheerful thought there, Maura.*

The rest of the day passed without any more incidents, and Carey came back into the inn in high spirits. Her eyes lit up when she saw the lampshade hovering in place of Mart's head. "Hi, Mart. New costume?"

"Yes, since someone stole my last one."

Luckily, Carey didn't hear that part. "Do you think it'd be better with Halloween lights instead?" I asked her.

"Yes... I wonder if we can find some." She pulled out her laptop with enthusiasm, and I gladly seized on the distraction to debate over what lights would be the most exciting for Mart to showcase on the tour next week. Every thought of the upcoming tour came with a spike of anxiety of what Halloween also represented, but I tamped down on my nerves for Carey's sake. Last night's ghost tour had been kind of low-key, as we were saving all the big stuff for next week.

Next week. When I also had to stop Mina. I wished those two things weren't inextricably tangled together.

When Allie came into the restaurant, I waylaid her. "Hey. Jia and I are going to meet up with some witches tonight, so is it okay if you and Carey take over the last part of our shift?"

"A coven meeting?" Her brow furrowed. "I didn't think the coven was in any state to hold gatherings after losing their leader."

"Not our coven," I clarified. "Priscilla and some of the ones who left. They've been hanging around near town in their own base."

"What, the witches who left the coven?" asked Carey. "They're still around?"

"Yep," I said. "They invited me to come and share information, and Jia offered to come with me."

"I suppose it's safer if you both go." Allie's gaze flickered to Carey, who was scribbling yet more ghost-tour costume ideas on a notepad. "Where's Drew?"

"Updating his team." He'd sent me a brief message saying that the others weren't best pleased when he'd dropped the news that they'd been looking in the wrong place for Mina, but I hadn't had the chance to talk to him properly since we'd left Greenwood Lake. I hoped they wouldn't insist on going to check themselves, though if Petra ended up getting herself hexed for trespassing in Isabella's hideout, it'd serve her right.

In any case, as little as I wanted to get my hopes up, this coven meeting might be my chance to figure out how to find Mina and stop her before Halloween. No, the witches wouldn't know what Mina had stolen from the Reapers or how she'd managed to kill one of them, but surely, Isabella at least knew what Mina had done during the floods. She knew what her former rival was capable of.

I figured Allie might suspect my real motives, but she refrained from saying so in front of her daughter. Like me, she didn't want to ruin the culmination of Carey's lifelong dreams by reminding her of the threat looming over our heads.

The witches might help. Or it might be a trap, but if I had Jia with me for moral support, they wouldn't do anything too heinous. I hoped.

# 6

Later that evening, Jia and I left the inn for the coven meeting. We'd discussed the merits of telling Wendy or someone else in the coven where we were going, just in case, but had decided against it. If any of the current coven members was secretly working for Mina—and the odds were high that at least one of them was—we didn't need to give them an opening.

I also hoped we didn't run into Mina herself, which was a possibility but not a strong one. She wouldn't see the need to risk blowing her own cover this close to Halloween when we'd made zero progress in actually finding her.

Mart declared that he wasn't going to come with us, which was probably for the best. Even bringing Jia along might be taken as a threat, but there was no chance I was showing up to a potentially hostile coven meeting without backup.

"Do you think they'll even show up?" Jia whispered as we walked out into the cold October night. "They might leave us to get stuck in their misdirection spells in the dark. I can see Isabella doing that."

"If she tries, I can probably find the way into their hideout using my Reaper abilities now that I know where to look."

"All right." Jia wore a dubious expression. "Here's hoping this isn't a dead end."

We both cast transportation spells that carried us into the darkened field in which I'd met the witches. At night, they didn't need concealment spells to effectively hide, and we hadn't taken two steps before we found ourselves surrounded by the glimmer of a dozen wands.

"You came." Isabella held up her wand to illuminate her disapproving face. "And brought a friend."

"An ally too," I corrected. "Jia has been against Mina from the start. She can help us."

"Nice to see you again," Jia said to Isabella. "I thought you left the country."

"You thought wrong." Isabella's tone was as icy as a frozen lake. "As a matter of fact, I thought the same of you."

If sparks had literally started flying between them, I wouldn't have been surprised. In retrospect, it should have been obvious that the pair wouldn't get along with one another.

"Hey, that's enough." Priscilla stepped into view, holding her own wand-light to illuminate the muddy field beneath our feet. "We should get indoors. It's not wise to draw attention to ourselves at night."

Isabella glared at Jia for a moment longer, and then she turned away. "Fine."

The cloaked witches walked across the field, their wands held aloft. A shimmer across my vision pointed me to the location of the misdirection spell, but the witches waved their wands in a complicated synchronised movement and continued walking.

They stopped to perform a similar movement twice more

before we reached a more solid-appearing shimmer that could only belong to a concealment spell. One wave of their wands later, and a building popped into existence. The walls were painted bright pink and magenta with golden unicorn motifs, like the aesthetic of the actual coven headquarters back in Hawkwood Hollow. The structure was so out of place amidst the fields that I wondered if someone had relocated their own home from elsewhere.

"Wow," Jia remarked. "So that's why you used a concealment spell. To keep from blinding everyone."

"Your sense of humour is as inappropriate as ever." Isabella pointed her wand at the door, which sprang open, and gestured for us to follow her into a narrow hallway. "Come on in before I change my mind."

The witches swept into the building, and Jia and I followed close behind Priscilla. The hallway's décor was equally eye-watering, the walls and carpet the same blinding shade of pink and decorated with yet more golden unicorn motifs. It was like walking into a haunted house owned by a Barbie afficionado.

We turned left off the hallway into a room packed with pointed hats, all of which swivelled towards us as we entered. I counted twenty witches in the room, which was more than I'd expected, though the staring I very much *had* expected. Since I was used to that, I ignored the whispers and sat down in a free seat. Jia sat next to me. Nobody spoke to us, but plenty of people spoke *about* us.

"It's the Reaper Witch."

"Who invited her?"

"She's going to doom us all."

*Well, this is fun.*

Isabella waited for the whispers to die down and then addressed the assembled witches. "You might have noticed we have two new additions to our number."

"She's joining our coven?" asked a pink-hatted witch who sounded disgusted at the very thought.

"I didn't know you *were* a coven," I retaliated, waving farewell to diplomacy. "Also, I'm not alone here. Jia's here too."

"That's right," said Jia. "I'd say I'm happy to see you all again, but... well."

Another wave of mutters arose, which Priscilla silenced by rising to her feet. "Maura has information for us on Mina's whereabouts."

"I never said that." Oh crap. "I thought *you* did. Out of interest, why are you hiding out here instead of working with the witches of Hawkwood Hollow?"

I already knew the answer to that, but this group of witches looked more like they had their sights set on a post-coven karaoke meeting than on hunting down and defeating their nemesis.

Yet more muttering ensued, but this time, Isabella didn't wait for them to quieten before she interrupted. "We were cast out of our coven long ago, thanks to Mina, and banded together for our own protection. We have no desire to return to those who supported her."

"Jennifer never supported her." I had to make that clear at least. "Am I to understand you've been hiding here as long as Mina's been on the run?"

"Yes," said one of the other witches. "We came together after she fled, but that doesn't mean she won't return to Hawkwood Hollow. That's why we haven't moved back."

"Some of us were glad to leave that place," the pink-hatted witch said. "The whole town gives me the creeps."

*That'll be because of Mina's ghosts.* How much did these witches know about Mina's role in the floods and the devastation that had followed? Some of them—like Isabella—were certainly old enough to remember the aftermath, since that was when Mina had seized power. It struck me that the town had probably looked very different beforehand.

"Then what's the point of all this?" Jia gave a sweeping gesture at the assembled witches. "We're trying to find Mina and take her out. I'd have thought you'd want the same."

"You want to take her on?" The pink-hatted witch laughed. "Good luck with that."

My shoulders tensed. "You seriously aren't bothered about her plans for world domination? You aren't going to be spared just because you're hiding under a few concealment spells, you know. Mina won't stand for any potential rivals lingering in the area."

"World domination?" The pink-hatted witch gave another laugh, this one more brittle than the first. "You're mad."

"Mina is," I corrected. "She plans to act on Halloween, you know. She told me herself."

"Didn't you tell anyone else?" Jia asked Priscilla. "Have you been keeping that to yourself?"

"I didn't get out of hospital that long ago," she said, sounding a tad abashed. "Besides, Mina never said *what* she planned to do on Samhain. Do you know anything more?"

"Nope." I didn't want to lay all my cards on the table when it was clear they *didn't* know where Mina was hiding, but I'd had enough of the mockery. "All I know is that her plans involve the afterworld."

The flurry of whispers that ensued gained a tenser edge. Isabella addressed me with genuine curiosity this time around. "Aren't you an expert on the afterworld?"

"Yes, but I'm not psychic," I told her. "Mina didn't give details, but she's sent monsters from the afterworld after me before, and Samhain is the night of the year when the veil between this world and the one beyond is at its thinnest. It's not hard to put two and two together."

The pink-hatted witch had stopped laughing. "Even Mina

wouldn't disrespect the sanctity of one of our most important nights of the year."

"She sent a vampiric serial killer after me a few weeks ago," I pointed out. "I doubt she cares much for sanctity."

A sharp intake of breath resounded, and several mutters of "vampire?" rippled around the room. Had Priscilla not even mentioned the man who'd nearly killed her? Not that Isabella was any better.

"Quiet!" she called to the room. "I'm sure Mina *claimed* she intended to act on a certain night, but it's equally plausible that she was trying to lure our quick-witted Reaper into a trap."

A ripple of laughter replaced the muttering, and angry heat rose to my face. "Trap or not, she's a murderer who deserves to be put away. Are you going to help me do it, or am I wasting my time by being here?"

"I don't recall agreeing to help you with anything." Isabella gave me a withering look. "I agreed to hear you out, but it seems all you have to give me is a lot of baseless speculation."

"Baseless?" I echoed. "I heard her claims with my own ears when I fought her."

"And lost, I assume," tittered the pink-hatted witch.

"Only because she made herself Reaper-proof." So much for not playing all my cards, but I had an inkling I would not be invited to any future coven meetings. Good riddance.

"Reaper-proof?" Isabella repeated. "What does that mean?"

"Well, the clue is in the name," I said caustically. "I couldn't touch her. Can't track her, either, which is the only reason I'm here instead of hunting her down myself."

"She must have got hold of one of those Reaper-proof spells," one of the witches said in a carrying whisper.

"What spells?" I asked sharply, pinpointing the speaker as

a grey-haired witch who wore a cloak in the same magenta shade as the décor. Maybe this was her house that Isabella and her friends had borrowed for their meetings. "You know of a Reaper-proof spell?"

Jia nudged me in the arm. "I bet that's why the other Reapers didn't find them."

*That's a possibility.* Dad had claimed Shelton just wasn't looking in the right place, but you'd think he'd have been able to sense the witches' presence at the very least. There'd have been no need for Drew's team to spend days traipsing through fields if he had.

"Right." I faced Priscilla. "What did you do, borrow Mina's spell to hide yourselves from me?"

A faint flush touched her face. "We didn't know if the Reapers were compromised or not."

"You don't know anything about the Reapers." I was aware that I sounded as snooty as the average council member, but I could hardly believe she'd had the nerve to steal Mina's own spell and use it against me. "Trust me when I say what Mina is going to do next week will have consequences far beyond the afterworld. If any of you want to help me stop her, now's the time to step up."

"That's right," Jia put in.

I gave her a look of gratitude.

But Isabella rose to her feet again. "No. You don't give orders to us."

"I'm not giving you orders. I'm stating my case." I readied myself to stand too. "Mina is dangerous. She'll happily wipe the lot of you off the map along with Hawkwood Hollow. You already said you outnumber her people, and you'll have an even bigger advantage if we join forces."

"I doubt it," Isabella said. "If what you said about her intentions on Samhain is right, you don't have an advantage at all."

"You're afraid of her." It was obvious, really, from the way they'd refused to go back to Hawkwood Hollow even after she'd been driven out of town. What was the point in going to such measures to hide themselves if they weren't scared half to death?

"You should be, too, Reaper Witch," the pink-hatted witch said.

"Doesn't mean we have to run away," I said. "Whatever she might have threatened you with, she's nothing but a petty bully who can't stand to lose. I don't run from petty bullies as a general rule."

"Nor I," added Jia. "She *did* threaten you, didn't she? That's why you left."

An undercurrent of unease permeated the room. Whispers pricked my ears, too quiet for me to make out the words. Had they learned of some of Mina's crimes or simply guessed at the murky circumstances in which she'd claimed the title of coven leader? All of the witches present in this room had been alive during the floods. Mina had erased the memories of the ghosts and ensured nobody ever spoke of the incident, but the sheer number of people who'd been forced out of town suggested that surely, *one* person in this room would know the truth.

I scanned the assembled witches and spied a frail-looking witch sitting across from me who wore an expression of barely concealed terror. When she saw me watching her, she huddled into her cloak and pulled her hat down over her face.

"You ran away, too, Jia," Isabella said to her. "You and the Reaper Witch have no right to act superior to us."

"I was a child, in case you've forgotten," Jia retaliated. "And Maura wasn't even here."

"I don't think there's anything wrong with running away," the pink-hatted witch announced. "She made threats, and she's perfectly capable of carrying them out, too, if she finds us."

"Does everyone in this room know what's at stake if Mina gets her way?" I infused my words with meaning, and Priscilla dropped her gaze, flushing harder.

"More than our lives?" Isabella retaliated. "What's your game, Reaper Witch?"

"To tell the truth about what Mina is capable of." I climbed to my feet and raised my voice, overriding the whispers. "Twenty years ago, Mina tried to open the door to the afterworld, and Harold the Reaper stopped her. Next week, she plans to try the same, and she's made herself invulnerable to Reapers to ensure nobody can get in her way this time. Do you think you'll be spared if you happen to be in the way of whatever she unleashes when she opens the afterworld?"

I waited, letting the impact of my words leap amongst the witches like a lit fuse. I'd laid down all my cards, but I had nothing left to lose at this point. Now they had the facts. Either they'd join me or they wouldn't. Nothing more I said would change their minds.

"Afterworld—what nonsense," the pink-hatted witch spluttered. "She's bluffing."

"You were all set on believing her earlier," another witch retaliated. "Wouldn't a Reaper know?"

"What makes her a Reaper? She doesn't even have a scythe."

*Okay, I think I've worn out my welcome.*

As the arguments intensified in volume, Priscilla beckoned Jia and me towards the door. With a final glance at the assembled witches, I crossed the circle and followed Priscilla into the hallway.

"Sorry," she whispered. "I could have told you they'd be resistant to offering to help."

"I thought they wanted Mina gone," I whispered back.

"Look, I know it sounds dire, but we *do* outnumber her. We have the entire police force of Hawkwood Hollow, Jia and some other witches, *and* three Reapers."

Four if my dad deigned to come and help and more if the Council showed up after all… but that was a possibility I preferred not to contemplate.

"Her vampire nearly killed me already," Priscilla said. "She's unpredictable, and as you kindly reminded the whole room, she nearly drowned the entire town twenty years ago."

"Being aware of that and refusing to do anything about it is the definition of cowardice," Jia said. "But I'd expect nothing else of the person who used Mina's dodgy spells to hide from accountability."

"That's not why I used the spell," Priscilla insisted. "Mina *did* deflect your Reaper powers, and I was concerned that meant the Reapers themselves were compromised. You can't tell me the thought never crossed your mind."

"It did, but you could have *asked* me." We approached the front door. "Didn't you even tell the others about Samhain? You heard her confession as clearly as I did."

"Not everyone in there is a regular coven attendee." She pushed open the door, and a gust of frigid wind swept inside. "In fact, this was our busiest meeting in weeks. Everyone wanted to meet the Reaper Witch."

Typical. "Well, it looks like they've decided they'd rather bicker amongst themselves than help."

"We don't have a consensus," she said. "You freaked everyone out by reminding them what Mina's capable of, but some of them will know you're right. I'll come to Hawkwood Hollow tomorrow and let you know what we decide on."

That would have to do. "I'll hold you to that."

"What a waste of time that was," Jia remarked as we stepped out into the chill night air. "Waste of concealment spells too."

"We did get some information." I watched Priscilla close the door behind us. "Namely, that Priscilla 'borrowed' Mina's Reaper-proofing spell to conceal herself from being detected."

"I'm not sure that's the same spell that blocked your scythe," Jia said. "I mean, if even the Reapers couldn't figure that one out, I doubt Priscilla managed to replicate the same spell that Mina used."

"Fair point."

Not wanting to linger too long, Jia and I used transportation spells to return to the inn.

As we landed outside, Shelton loomed up out of the darkness. I yelped and jumped backwards into a puddle.

"Whoa!" Jia startled. "What was that in aid of?"

"I've been contacted by another Reaper," Shelton said to me. "He claims to have information for you."

I put a hand to my racing heart. "You didn't need to scare the crap out of us like that."

"I didn't know you were going to appear out of thin air," he retorted. "He wants to talk to you as soon as possible."

"Who wants to talk to me?" I'd had a night of it already. "Which Reaper? Not someone from the Council."

"No," he said cryptically. "Come on."

I nodded to Jia, indicating for her to go back to the inn alone. "Fine, but this better be good."

While Jia departed for the cosy warmth of the inn, I reluctantly followed Shelton into the chill darkness of the afterworld.

A moment later, we emerged on a night-darkened path. When I spotted the hooded figure approaching us, tension zipped up my spine. *Which Reaper is this?*

The Reaper pushed down his hood, revealing a startlingly young face, curly blond hair, and blue eyes.

"Oh," I said. "It's you, Xavier."

# 7

Xavier looked at me in equal surprise. "It's you. Maura."

"Who else would it be?" I turned to Shelton and then back to Xavier. "What are you doing all the way up north?"

Xavier and I had met in the magical library of Ivory Beach. We'd got along about as well as one would expect, considering one of us was a rogue Reaper and one a rule-following apprentice. Which was to say he wanted to have me hauled in for interrogation, and his delightful boss had nearly done exactly that. What was he doing all the way out here?

"I heard about your rogue witch," he said. "Including her plans for Halloween."

"Who told you that?" I glanced at Shelton, already guessing the source. "I didn't know you were acquainted."

"Reapers talk to one another," Xavier replied. "You hinted at your little problem when you came to visit the library, so I decided to find out more."

"There's a reason I haven't told the Council," I warned.

"This place is a stick of dynamite waiting to go off. I don't want them to show up and set off the fuse without catching the person responsible for putting it there."

I'd tried not to give too much away to anyone I met during my trip to Ivory Beach, but ultimately, the reason I'd been visiting the library in the first place had been to find out a way to stop Mina and work out how she'd managed to block my Reaper powers. It wouldn't have been hard for a curious Reaper apprentice to work out the rest.

"I gathered," he said. "My boss took a bit of convincing to let me to come here, so I can't stay long."

"I'm surprised he agreed at all." The guy put the "Grim" in "Grim Reaper." "What's this information you have? If it's that Mina probably stole from the Reaper Council with the aid of the Founders, we already worked that out."

"Did you?" His expression showed little surprise. "What exactly do you think she stole?"

"I don't know, but she already devised an anti-Reaper booby trap spell of a sort, and this seems to be a more powerful variation of the same spell."

"She didn't steal from the Reaper Council," Xavier said. "I've checked, and there's nothing officially created by the Reapers that would allow a human to best one of us."

"How'd you figure that one out?" I frowned. "You didn't tell me that when I came to visit the library. Neither did your boss."

"He's the one who found out," said Xavier. "Our only conclusion was that Mina obtained the means of opposing us from her Founder contacts. The Founders are known to have experimented with creating their own spells and devices for various purposes."

"Usually unpleasant ones." I suppressed a shiver. "You think that's where she got the spell?"

"Yes, and your friend Shelton agrees with me."

He didn't have to rub it in. "Well, she *did* steal from the Reaper Council when she killed one of them."

Xavier grimaced. "I didn't know *that* when I came here, but I wouldn't have thought a mere talisman would have given her that much of an edge over a fully trained Reaper. I don't know what kind of object the Founders made."

"She'll have even more of an edge now that she has access to a volume of demonic magic." Another shiver rose to my skin. "That's what she stole."

"I would guess that she's already consulted the book," Shelton growled. "She owned it for years, after all, but this makes it all the more urgent that we prevent whatever she plans to do on Halloween."

*Figures.* "The witches… they're no use. Priscilla didn't even tell her allies about Mina's plans, and they flew into a panic when I told them."

"I thought so," Shelton said. "No, we won't get any help from the witches. This is on us."

"Meaning the Reapers?" I raised a brow at him. "Did you forget she's Reaper-proofed? Nobody even knows where she's hiding."

"There's a way to find her hiding place," said Shelton. "She might have Reaper-proofed herself, but she's been using the afterworld, and any contact with the other side leaves traces that a Reaper can follow."

"Really?" I furrowed my brow. "So… you can track the place she's been using to contact the afterworld? What if she's anticipated that and is using another location to communicate with the other side?"

"She might be," said Shelton, "but I doubt it. She'll want to keep her allies close at hand. Human and otherwise."

"Lovely." He might well be right, but if I'd never covered that kind of use of my Reaper skills in my apprenticeship, it must have been an advanced tactic. "That sounds like the kind of thing the Reaper Council would disapprove of."

Shelton gave a snort. "You, Maura, have never cared a jot for the Reaper Council's disapproval in your life."

He'd got me there. "Dad would disapprove too."

"That's why I already got his permission."

Ah. So that was what they'd been discussing at the Reaper's house. "When did you plan to act? Because the instant we get Mina's attention, that's it."

"Not necessarily," said Xavier. "It sounds as though it'll work in her favour to hold back until Halloween. If we take her by surprise before then, we might be able to get the upper hand."

"We have to act soon," I concluded. "Priscilla said she'd drop by the inn as soon as the witches had come to an agreement, but that doesn't mean we'll be able to count on their help. It'll be a lot easier to corner Mina if we can get her surrounded."

"According to the police, your first priority should be rescuing the coven leader," Shelton said. "If you corner Mina first, there's a chance she might try to use the coven leader as a shield."

"Jennifer." My throat went dry. "I don't know if she's even alive."

"A coven leader would work as potential leverage," said Xavier. "But this Mina seems unpredictable."

"That's an understatement." Mina *would* use Jennifer as a shield given the chance, and I didn't know that I could live with Jennifer's death on my conscience. Yet if I had to choose between that and stopping Mina from opening the afterworld and enacting a repeat of the floods, what was I supposed to do? "There's no reason we can't rescue Jennifer *and* bring Mina to justice."

"Can you take her on?" Shelton enquired. "Do you believe you can beat her?"

*No. Yes.* "If I get her Reaper-proof protection away from her... maybe I can."

"You're assuming it'll be easy to remove," Shelton said. "If she's wearing a simple talisman, she'll have taken other precautions, and most of our usual tricks won't work on her."

"Like dragging her into the afterworld," I surmised. "Yeah. We won't know until we see her in person, though."

"Exactly," Xavier put in. "She's an unknown. My boss told me to tread carefully, but he doesn't know she's capable of killing a Reaper. If he knew, he'd have ordered me to return home."

I wondered if he'd told Rory he was here. He must have, surely, and she and the Grim Reaper would have been in agreement on that point if they knew how precarious the situation was. "If you're still in, when do you want to try reaching her?"

Part of me wanted to take her on here and now, but I was already exhausted from the upheaval of the past day, and we needed a clearer plan than "make a racket in the afterworld and get Mina's attention." Not to mention Drew would appreciate knowing too.

"I'll be in touch tomorrow," said Shelton. "We're both staying at a hostel in Littlewood."

"I did wonder," I said. "I figured you weren't staying at the inn, considering it's full of even more ghosts than it usually is."

"Why's that?" Xavier asked.

"Halloween, remember?" I said. "Anyway, half the town's inhabitants are ghosts, and they can barely tolerate *one* Reaper being around, and that's only because I've helped so many of them."

"Yes... I won't mention *that* part to my boss," Xavier said. "You're playing a dangerous game."

"Me?" I raised a brow at him. "I might remind you that it's Mina's fault the whole town is flooded with ghosts. She killed them, and she'll happily do the same thing again in a few days if we don't stop her first. I'd say that's worth risking a trip into the afterworld."

---

Despite my bold proclamations, I slept horribly that night and was plagued by dreams of Mina chasing me with a scythe. I woke in a cold sweat to the sound of Mart's out-of-tune singing. He'd reacted to my update on Shelton and Xavier's plan with little more than a shrug, though that might have been due to his annoyance at being left out of our "top-secret Reaper meeting."

"I didn't think you'd appreciate me yanking you through the afterworld to join in," I said to him as we walked down to the lobby. "I also had no idea it would be Xavier who Shelton had invited to join him. I guess the Reapers really do talk to one another."

"Except you."

"Thanks." I decided to let that one slide. Reaching the lobby, I waved at Allie, who was helping yet another set of guests check in at the front desk. I didn't see any new ghostly intruders, but the group of spirits I'd spotted the previous day had joined the other newcomers in the restaurant.

I shooed them away from the buffet table. "Stop that. You'll make the food go cold."

The ghosts obeyed, though their gazes lingered on me, and a gangly teenage ghost actually reached out to touch my arm.

"Hey!" I took a sharp step back. "What was that for?"

"He was checking to see if you were really a Reaper," said one of his friends.

"Well, don't." I gave Mart a warning look when he started to snicker to himself. "If I wasn't a Reaper, I wouldn't tolerate you lot relocating here."

"Wouldn't you?" The teenage ghost surveyed me. "I thought you were a protector of the dead."

"Who told you that?"

He shrugged a lanky shoulder. "Rumours. Everyone in the afterworld calls you that."

"They'd bloody better not." I glowered at the retreating ghosts and then smoothed out my expression when a group of actual *living* guests walked into the restaurant.

Mart cackled. "Protector of the dead. Should we put that on your uniform?"

I rolled my eyes and helped myself to breakfast. Carey soon came to join me, full of curious questions about the witches who lived outside of Hawkwood Hollow that I answered with as much honesty as I could. She'd been in bed by the time I returned to the inn after my meeting with the Reapers, and I omitted that last part from my story. Jia knew, and I'd sent Drew a message, but I needed to speak to him later to make sure his team was on board with the other Reapers' plan.

*Five days until Halloween*, the gleaming banner Carey had affixed to the wall proclaimed. The number was enchanted to change of its own accord each day until Halloween, and I hadn't the heart to tell her that seeing the number filled me with dread rather than excitement. When Carey set off for school, I got out my wand and surreptitiously covered the banner with a cloaking spell.

"Hey, I wanted to keep track of what day it is," Mart objected.

"You know perfectly well what day it is." I waved at Jia,

who'd just walked into the restaurant. "I don't need a screaming reminder that we have five days to stop Mina's apocalypse glowing on the wall."

"Didn't the Reapers help?" Jia wore a red scarf patterned with cartoon cats wearing pointed hats today. "I thought that Xavier had a plan."

"It's more Shelton's plan than his, but it's a risk wrapped in a gamble."

"So the same as all your plans."

She'd got me there. "This one hinges on something that'll really tick off the Council if they find out."

"Again, that's not all that out of the ordinary for you." Her eyes glittered with amusement. "Is it something I can help with?"

"Not sure *I'll* be much use," I admitted. "Shelton doesn't have a lot of confidence in me. Neither do Isabella and her friends."

"The same witches who've been sitting in a bunker for decades?" Jia pursed her lips. "You can run circles around the lot of them *without* your Reaper powers. Priscilla is the only one with any real skill, and the vampire got the best of her."

"You don't think the witches are actually going to help, do you?" Mart asked. "Hey, new ghosts."

I stifled a groan, spying several newcomers clustering in the lobby. "Aren't they from Hawkwood Hollow?"

"Yes," Mart said. "I wonder if they think you're the Ghost Protector too."

*Lucky Xavier didn't come here. And Shelton.* Though given the ghosts' fixation on my supposed protector status, they might have been as unbothered by the other Reapers as they were by the sage all over the ground outside.

"The *what?*" Jia said. "Ghost Protector? Is that your new title?"

"According to the other ghosts, it is." Mart snickered.

"No way," I said firmly. "I don't need any more pressure on my head."

"It's not pressure, though," Jia said. "You just protect the ghosts by default. It's what you do."

"This place is full of more sage than an apothecary."

"And yet they're still here." She gently prodded me in the arm. "That's the point I'm making. They trust *you*."

"Based on a rumour." I dropped the subject. "Never mind the ghosts. Do you think Priscilla will keep her word and come back today?"

"Not likely," said Jia. "She's lost her nerve since the vampire nearly skewered her. And the other witches never had much nerve to begin with."

"That's what I figured." I stifled a yawn behind my hand. "I need to speak to Drew, but I don't know that the police should get involved in the Reapers' plan either. It's not like they can see the afterworld."

I messaged Drew, who said he'd drop by at lunchtime to discuss strategies, and then busied myself preparing for the day's shift.

Priscilla did not show up that morning, and lunchtime rolled around with the usual flood of customers. Luckily, most of them were ghosts, and the spirits' attempts to buy hot cocoa with invisible money ended in Jia humouring them by setting out a single mug on the counter for them to cluster around so they could savour the warmth.

When Drew showed up, I took my lunch break and joined him at a free table.

"How many ghosts are in here?" he asked, watching Jia converse with what to him would have looked like thin air.

"Too many," I said. "It's lucky for them that Shelton and Xavier are staying in Littlewood instead."

"Xavier," he repeated. "He's the Reaper you met in... Ivory Beach?"

"The apprentice Reaper," I confirmed. "His boss is less friendly, though he refrained from reporting me to the Council in the end."

"And he sent Xavier to help you?"

"I think Xavier sent himself," I replied. "He and Shelton have a plan to get Mina's attention and lure her out into the open. I'm waiting for them to confirm when."

His eyes widened. "Do you want me to tell my team?"

"I don't know," I admitted. "I mean, it depends on whether your team wants to sign on to a plan that might blow up in our faces."

"Since she's killed one Reaper, it's a good idea to bring some non-Reapers with you," he said. "What about those witches?"

"Priscilla hasn't shown her face here yet." I picked up a sandwich from the plate that had appeared on our table, courtesy of Allie. "I don't hold out much hope that she'll volunteer."

"What about the locals?" he asked. "Jennifer's allies, I mean."

I shook my head. "Too risky. Aside from Wendy, who isn't exactly a fighter, we don't know which of them might be reporting back to Mina."

"True," he said. "All right. I'll talk to the team—"

The doors blew open, drawing our attention. I expected another entourage of ghosts, but instead, Priscilla walked into the restaurant.

"She did show up." I rose to my feet and went to meet her. "Did you come to a consensus?"

"Once the other witches stopped arguing, they agreed that some of us need to volunteer to fight Mina."

"I have an update for you too," I told her. "Another Reaper is in the area—not with the Council—and we believe we can lure Mina out into the open."

Her face paled. "How?"

"Using the afterworld," I replied, keeping my voice low. "Mina's been colluding with the other side in some way, and it'll have left traces behind that a Reaper can follow, regardless of whatever spell she's used to hide herself."

"Why not do that yourself?" she asked. "I thought you were an expert."

*More than you are.* "Only official Reapers are allowed to do that sort of thing. If it works, though… do you want to come confront her?"

Fear flickered in her eyes. "If she *has* been liaising with the afterworld, this is way beyond us. We'd die."

"I thought you and some of the others wanted to help out."

"Not with unnecessary risks."

"You signed up to help a Reaper," I pointed out. "And to fight against someone who's using the Reapers' skills without oversight and without real understanding of what she's doing. If you didn't want to deal with the afterworld, you should have toppled her from her position when she was a simple coven leader."

"She was never a mere coven leader," Priscilla said. "I thought you of all people would know that."

"Well, the Reapers are our only shot at stopping her." Jia strode to my side. "And Maura. Are you in or not?"

"You haven't given me all the details," Priscilla said. "Say your plan forces her out into the open… what then?"

"We grab Jennifer, remove Mina's anti-Reaper talisman or whatever it is, and hopefully get her in handcuffs."

"That sounds like wishful thinking to me," Priscilla said. "She'll be prepared for anything, I guarantee."

"It's that or wait until Samhain," I said. "Are you in?"

She gulped. "Provisionally. I'll let the others know."

"I'll need your phone number," said Jia. "Well?"

Priscilla reluctantly mumbled a string of numbers and then left, looking as though she thoroughly regretted signing up to a Reaper's plan.

"You'll have to be the one to message her," I said to Jia. "I still have my phone on silent because of my mother."

"I'll text her when you're ready," Jia said. "I'm laying bets that she won't show up, though."

I returned to our table, where Drew sat, watching the door. "I hope she's trustworthy," he said.

"Me too," I murmured. "But if we can't trust each other, what else is there to do?"

# 8

Word from the Reapers arrived just before closing time, in the form of Shelton materialising behind the counter and scaring the crap out of Jia, me, and the nearby ghosts. He stopped only long enough to say, "Meet me at the Reaper's house in an hour," and then he vanished.

*Here goes nothing.*

Jia sent a message to Priscilla as planned, while I told Allie we were off. Her reaction was anxiety mixed with support. She knew what was at stake if we failed to stop Mina before Halloween.

Since we wouldn't all be able to fit inside Harold's cottage, I walked there with Jia and asked Drew and his team to meet us outside. When we reached the cottage, however, we found the door closed and Shelton and Xavier standing on the other side of the cemetery gates.

"Let me guess… he's not coming?" I indicated the Reaper's cottage.

Shelton grunted. "Did you expect him to?"

"I can see how this place ended up being infested with ghosts," Xavier remarked. "That guy's your local Reaper."

"I can hear you talking about me," the door growled.

I stepped closer. "Out of interest, why *not* come and help us?"

The door opened a fraction, revealing Harold's face. "You can't beat someone who can deflect a Reaper's scythe. You'll be lucky to walk away with your life."

"Did Shelton tell you everything?" I asked. "If he did, you'll know that we have a plan. We also have the entire police team, several witches, and three Reapers. Four if you come too."

"If you all die in there, who will protect the people of Hawkwood Hollow?"

I bit back a sarcastic comment to the effect that he'd made very little effort in that direction for most of the time I'd known him. It'd be unfair of me to say so, but he didn't have to undermine my confidence in our plan when I'd need every ounce of courage possible.

Harold narrowed his eyes in a way that suggested he'd caught the gist of my thoughts, and he made to close the door.

"If we don't stop Mina, nobody will be safe, living or dead." I stuck my foot in the doorway. "If you aren't going to help, can I borrow your scythe?"

He all but shoved the curved instrument into my hands before closing the door on me, properly this time. It was not an auspicious sign for our upcoming battle, but it couldn't be helped. Retreating from the door, I joined the others beside the cemetery gate.

"Harold's staying behind?" Drew guessed.

"Yeah, he's sitting this one out." I hefted the scythe. "Let's go."

The blood surged in my veins. This was it.

While the two Reapers travelled through the afterworld to the designated waiting spot outside of Hawkwood Hollow, I remained with the humans, using a combination of transportation spells to reach the countryside at the town's border.

Nobody else was waiting for us. I checked my phone, but even Dad hadn't messaged me that morning. Mum had but not with anything consequential. She just wanted to know when I'd next come visit. *When we aren't preventing the apocalypse*, I wanted to reply.

"I knew Priscilla wouldn't show up," Jia said. "Her allies must have had second thoughts."

"I'll find them," said Mart and vanished into the afterworld.

I waited, the Reapers on one side of me, Drew's team on the other, and Jia standing awkwardly in the middle. *Did Priscilla chicken out?*

Mart returned within minutes. "She's not in the area," he announced. "I'd say she got cold feet."

"We can't stand out here forever," growled Shelton.

When the Reapers began to walk away, I turned to Drew and his team. "Do you want to do this now? Without Priscilla and her allies?"

"It doesn't look like we have much choice," Jia remarked. "I figured she'd bail on us."

"What do you want us to do?" Drew eyed the retreating Reapers. "You'll have to tell us if there's anything we're supposed to be looking at. Nobody on my team can see ghosts."

"I know." A spasm of dread clutched me. Maybe I should have urged him to stay behind, but it was unreasonable to expect Drew to stand back and let me go off to fight Mina alone.

I wished he hadn't brought the entire team with him as

well. At least Petra wasn't amongst the group of wizards and shifters who'd accompanied him out into the field, but even experienced police officers were at a disadvantage when faced with the dead.

*They volunteered for this*, I told myself. *Besides, Mina isn't dead. Unfortunately.*

We continued to walk. I wanted to put as much distance between us and the town as possible in case our attempts to track Mina ended in her chasing us down, but the mere act of drawing her attention would put Hawkwood Hollow at risk. I'd known that going in, but now, I couldn't suppress a spike of panic when darkness cloaked the hillside. The two Reapers were barely visible to my eyes.

"What are you doing?" I called to them.

Shelton and Xavier didn't answer. They stood in a halo of darkness, scythes held aloft, and I lifted my own borrowed scythe as I strode to join them.

"Please tell me one of you is doing that." I gestured to the sweeping darkness. "Out of interest, how does this spell of yours work? What do you do, ask the afterworld to give you directions to the place where Mina is communicating with the other side? Or do we just... jump straight in?"

"The latter," said Shelton. "Once I've established a link."

"What—you want me to bring the entire police team through the afterworld?" I glanced over my shoulder at Drew, who'd frozen, and so had Jia. "That wasn't in the job description."

"It's not my job to pander to sightless humans." He faced the darkness and spoke several words in a language I didn't understand.

"Get ready," Xavier said over his shoulder.

"Hey!" I ran back to Jia and the others. "Shelton is under the impression that you're willing to jump through the afterworld into Mina's hideout."

"What's he doing?" Jia furrowed her brow. "I... I can *see* the afterworld. Is that supposed to happen?"

"I hope so, because so can I." Drew had gone tense, and the hint of a growl underlaid his voice.

I'd hardly taken a step before the darkness came alive. A huge shaggy form emerged from the gloom, barrelling straight towards us.

I swiped with the scythe and missed as the beast leapt, sailing straight over my head. Mart yelped and vanished as a second shaggy form followed the first, jaws agape and slavering.

*Is that the thing that killed the Reaper?* I ran at the second beast, but that one dodged my scythe too. It was surprisingly nimble for its size, and in the ensuing chaos, the police team had scattered into the surrounding dark. Xavier came sprinting towards the monster, his scythe at the ready.

"Shelton, what the hell was that?" I yelled in the other Reaper's general direction. "You were supposed to take us to Mina, not summon her monsters here."

*Jia. Drew.* I couldn't see them at all behind the darkness cloaking the field, though I heard growling and snarling that distinctly belonged to a werewolf and not one of Mina's monsters.

As a third beast materialised, I launched into a sprint and ran headlong into Shelton's back. He caught his balance, continuing his muttering in an unfamiliar language and seemingly oblivious to the chaos erupting around us.

"Why are you reciting Latin poetry at a time like this?" I yelled in his ear.

"It's not *poetry*," he said through his teeth. "It's a Reaper tracking spell. I'm after the source of those monsters."

"Were you intending to summon them on top of us?"

Shelton resumed chanting without answering my question, while I engaged the third monster with my scythe. I could only assume Mart had gone to hide somewhere out of their reach, and I couldn't say I blamed him in the slightest. The beast roared, sending icy waves of foul breath over my face, as my scythe sank into its side.

The sensation was more like plunging a knife into smoke than stabbing a solid creature, but the beast's roar was real enough. My ears burned, and when I released the scythe, the monster exploded into a column of ashes.

Shelton hadn't even stopped his recital in order to lend me a hand. I could only assume he was ploughing ahead with his plan to track the source of the monsters through the afterworld, but it was obvious that Mina had been expecting some kind of interference. That or the monsters were a test run for her plans on Halloween.

Shelton's chanting grew louder. The darkness surrounding him took on an odd glowing quality.

"Don't you dare!" I sprinted towards him and into the glowing patch of darkness, which swallowed both of us up.

I closed my eyes to block out the glow, feeling myself tumbling through the afterworld. Shelton's chanting had ceased, and a roaring in my ears was the only sound before my back hit solid carpeted floor with a thud.

I groaned. Blinking the glare from my eyes, I looked up at a bewildered Jennifer Ness. Her usually impeccably styled blond hair was lank and greasy, her face pale and stained with dirt, but it was definitely her.

"*Maura?*"

"That's me." I lifted my head. "Where am I? In Mina's bolt-hole?"

Her eyes bulged. "She'll find you. She'll kill you."

"She can try." I rose to my feet, examining my surroundings. The room was tiny, more like a cupboard, and Shelton didn't seem to have followed me inside. He must have landed somewhere else. Hopefully on top of Mina.

Jennifer leaned against the wall for balance. Her face was deathly pale, and she looked as though she might keel over. "Maura… you're really here."

"What did she do to you?" I reached for the scythe, which had landed on the floor beside me, and tried the door handle with my other hand. My teeth shook in my skull as a sharp shock travelled up my arm. Ow. Well. That answered the question of whether she'd Reaper-proofed the place or not.

How was I supposed to get out of here now? I pushed the door again, but it didn't give. *Why did I have to land* inside *the prison?* "Why'd she keep you alive?"

"She'll kill you," Jennifer mumbled without answering my question. "You've doomed us both."

"Not quite." She might have had a point, though. Jennifer could barely walk as it was, and it was only a matter of time before Mina realised I'd accidentally landed next to her prisoner. If Shelton had distracted her, it would help, but that was assuming she didn't have worse than those monsters up her sleeve.

Hefting the scythe, I swung it at the door with all my strength.

An unseen *force* pushed back, but the door trembled in its frame. Sparks flew outward, and my teeth rattled again when a second shock pierced my bones. *Ouch.*

"You can't!" Jennifer squeaked. "This place is protected against Reapers. Now that you've touched that door, you can't use your powers."

"I can use this." I gave another swing, and this time, the door shook so hard that I heard a sharp snapping noise, like something breaking.

Then footsteps rang out. *Oh crap. Guess I drew her attention.*

I took a step back then another. The door swung open, and Mina stood on the other side. No sign of Shelton.

I tried for a smile. "You know, this isn't exactly how I expected this to go."

No Reaper powers. No other way out except the door behind her. I had my scythe, though I wasn't any the wiser as to how she'd Reaper-proofed herself. I couldn't see her wearing any kind of talisman around her neck, but she might have concealed it elsewhere.

Her gaze passed over my scythe. "That won't work on me, Maura. This little rescue mission will only end in your death."

"It's not a rescue mission." I released the scythe with one hand, which I plunged into my pocket, and swung one-handed at her head.

The scythe bounced off her, but I'd expected it to. My free hand drew my wand out of my pocket, and I used it to cast an immobilisation spell.

My spell bounced off her, but she didn't draw her own wand in return. What had she done, shielded herself? Wishing she'd move out of the doorway, I backed further into the room, positioning myself in front of Jennifer.

"Aren't you going to use your wand?" I queried. "Or would you rather just stand there and let everything bounce off you?"

Holding the scythe in my left hand was incredibly awkward, but I wasn't about to let go of my weapon, and I didn't have a sheath to store it in. I kept my wand in my dominant hand and tried another spell, which also fizzled out.

"You're wasting your time, Maura," said Mina. "I'm far beyond your reach."

"You're right in front of my nose." She must have had gaps in her defences somewhere. Maybe I could stall her until Shelton showed up, but she must have known a second Reaper had landed in her house too.

"You have no idea what I'm capable of, Maura." Her voice became distorted. So did her face, which twisted into a wide grin that looked unnatural on her. Her eyes turned flat black, as if the pupils had expanded, and gained a smoky quality.

My blood iced over. She was possessed. She'd *already* summoned a demon, and now her indifference made a horrible kind of sense. The demon had couched itself inside her body—which was already Reaper-proofed—and while I might have assumed it'd overpowered her will, Mina was not the sort to do anything by accident.

"Did you... *let* the demon possess you?" I wasn't even sure if I was talking to Mina or to the demon, but usually, the demon won out over its human host. Usually. But because Mina was such a powerful witch, they might have come to some kind of arrangement.

*What level of demon is it, though?*

Mina spoke again in that odd, distorted voice. "You're not strong enough a Reaper to beat me, Maura."

She lifted her hand, and I flew through the air. My back slammed into the wall, the air flew from my lungs, and the scythe dropped from my hands. My vision swam, doubling, making it seem as though two Minas advanced on me, possessed by two demons.

*This is how I'm going to die? Really?*

A figure moved at the edge of my vision. Jennifer, making a run for it while she could. I didn't really blame her, but a spike of alarm rose when the demon—or Mina—raised a hand for a second time.

Sparks flew, causing Mina to step back. Jennifer had picked up my discarded wand, and while her aim was way off, she'd saved my life. In Mina's split second's hesitation, I rolled out of the line of fire.

Then Shelton ran into the room.

# 9

When Shelton entered, Mina turned on him with a snarl. Jennifer came running to help me to my feet. I took my wand back from her with a whispered "Thanks," hoping she'd take a hint and flee. I then grabbed the fallen scythe and made to join Shelton in facing off against Mina.

"No," Shelton said out of the corner of his mouth. "Leave."

*You can't win,* he meant, and the grimness in his eyes told me he'd figured out the truth of our dilemma. Mina had already summoned a demon, and their combined forces had already killed one Reaper. With my abilities cut off, I'd be a liability even with a scythe.

Yet… I couldn't leave him to fight Mina alone.

The demon spoke through her mouth. "I'll kill all of you."

Shelton gestured at the door again. "Get *out,* Maura."

And he ran at her, swinging his scythe. As expected, his weapon bounced off Mina as though she was surrounded by an invisible shield. *What kind of spell is she using?* It must have had a limit, and while she might be Reaper-proof and witch-proof, she wasn't plain-old-human-proof.

I pushed the scythe into a startled Jennifer's hands and tackled Mina from behind. She staggered, losing her balance, and Shelton caught her by the scruff of her neck. Her hands flailed, and I glimpsed a gleaming ring on one finger. That was new. *She's not married, is she?*

The gleam gained a shimmering sheen, and the penny dropped.

"Hey!" I shouted, gearing up to tackle her again.

Shadows oozed out of Mina's body, and Shelton let go of her as though burned. Recovering, she lunged at him, and he sidestepped, eyes narrowed in fury. "Maura, I told you—"

"You need a *hand*," I retaliated, putting emphasis on the last word. Triumph stirred when his gaze caught on the gleaming ring on her finger. Her talisman.

Unfortunately, that was when Mina spun around and grabbed me by the throat.

I gagged, choking, hands reaching to pry her loose. Shadows oozed up my neck, and a chill numbed my skin. My fingers twitched, trying to grasp the ringed finger.

A thud resounded, and Mina let go of me. Jennifer stood behind her, her eyes wild and the scythe in her hands. While the scythe itself had bounced off its target, she'd had the surprisingly helpful idea of striking Mina in the back of the head with the hilt. Shelton was ready, and in a fluid motion, he seized Mina's hand and pulled the ring free.

"You!" The shriek that erupted from Mina was definitely her own voice, not the demon's, but the shadows that surged over Shelton undeniably belonged to the latter. They closed around his legs, rooting him to the spot.

*He shouldn't have a problem with that,* I thought—but his eyes had widened, and he gave yet another furious gesture towards the door.

"Run." He swung his fist, and the ring came sailing towards me.

I raised a hand, caught the ring, and then finally obeyed Shelton's signal to run. As I did, Mina gave another shriek and lunged forward.

I didn't see what happened next. As I reached the door, Jennifer slammed it closed from the other side.

"Come on!" she gasped.

"Dammit, Shelton," I called to the closed door. "You'd better be close behind me."

I let Jennifer overtake me, following a narrow landing to a staircase. Due to the lack of windows in Jennifer's prison, I hadn't even known we were upstairs, but I didn't have time to stop and scan our surroundings. With the ring clenched in one hand, I followed Jennifer downstairs to a door and kicked it open.

When we burst outside into daylight, a surge of regret hit me. *Shelton.* Reapers were supposed to be immune to demons, but he was fighting Mina in close quarters, and his obvious panic suggested that the demon was stronger than he'd expected. That or he'd walked into the anti-Reaper defences and had his powers cut off. The last thing I wanted to do was leave him to handle her alone, but even the two of us were collectively outclassed, and someone had to help Jennifer get out of here. She sagged against the wall, her expression more exhausted than I'd ever seen her. "Didn't any of the other witches come with you?" she asked.

"No," I said. "Priscilla and her friends were supposed to help, but I guess they were all talk."

I felt bad that none of her fellow witches had volunteered to come to her rescue either, but my other allies had been left behind when Shelton and I had jumped through the afterworld, and I'd unintentionally left them fighting Mina's monsters.

Jennifer took a shaky step forward. "She... took my wand. I can't get us out of here."

"I'll get you home." I lifted my wand and pictured Hawkwood Hollow, intentionally aiming at Jennifer, not at myself. As she vanished, my gaze went to the house, but the upstairs room in which I'd left Shelton had no windows.

*He wants me to get rid of this ring.* And thanks to whatever spell Mina had used on the door, I couldn't access the afterworld.

Cursing under my breath, I cast a second transportation spell on myself, picturing the field I'd left behind.

My feet touched down on wet grass, and Xavier exclaimed when I landed behind him. "Maura. I thought you went with…"

"Shelton." I spun around, seeing that the darkness had receded and that the monsters had gone too. "He's fighting her. Mina. Where's Drew? And Jia?"

"Maura!" Jia came running over to me. "Drew's been trying to deal with those monsters, but they keep getting up again."

"We need someone to banish them." Monsters from the afterworld were resilient, but they weren't the real danger we'd face if Mina came back.

"I'll handle it." Xavier swore. "If Mina's occupied fighting Shelton, and she's not coming here…"

"I wouldn't count on it." I clenched my fist around the ring, and a sudden wave of dizziness hit me.

"What did she do to you?" Jia peered at my face.

"Nothing." I held up a shaking hand. "She Reaper-proofed her hideout. Shelton's stuck in there, fighting her."

"Shelton can take care of himself," said Jia firmly. "Drew—she's here."

A growling drew my attention to Drew, who came bounding over in his werewolf form. While Xavier ran to banish the monsters, I held out my hand to reveal Mina's ring.

"What's that?" Jia's eyes widened. "That's... a talisman. Was she using that to Reaper-proof herself?"

"Yes, and we'd better hope she doesn't desperately want it back." The dizziness hit me again. Was the ring affecting me because it was supposed to work against Reapers?

Jia snatched the ring from my hand. "We'll destroy this. It's not indestructible, I'm willing to bet."

The dizziness faded a little, and a faint sense of alarm trickled in. "Mart... where's Mart?"

"I thought he went to hide when it all kicked off." Jia pocketed the ring. "What, you don't think it affected him as well?"

"I hope not." I clenched my fist, where the ring had left a cold imprint on my hand. "Can you take the anti-Reaper spell off me?"

"Of course." Jia got out her wand, and in a flash, the afterworld returned to my perception.

Mart loomed out of the darkness, paler than before but very much present. "You told me you wouldn't run off alone," he accused.

"Did I?" While my dizziness receded, a sense of despair settled over me. "You know, it doesn't matter that we got her anti-Reaper talisman. Mina's already summoned a higher demon. And I think they're working together."

---

Mina did not come running to fetch the ring. Maybe she'd figured we'd destroy it right away, which would have been my plan. If Xavier hadn't objected.

"I'll take it to Harold," he told me as our bedraggled group gathered to return to Hawkwood Hollow. "He'll want to see it."

"Given up on Shelton already?" Guilt constricted my throat. "I don't want to *leave* him there."

"You're in no shape to fight," Jia told me firmly. "Also, it sounds like Shelton was determined for you to leave. He knew what he was doing."

"Exactly," Xavier said. "He's the reason I'm even here, but he's a stronger Reaper than either of us. You want to protect your town too. Right?"

"Right." Hawkwood Hollow needed me too.

While Xavier went to the Reaper's cottage, the police headed back to their office. Except for Drew, who was still in werewolf form and remained close to me as though he suspected I might run off to fight Mina if he turned his back.

"I'm going back to the inn," I told him. "Do you want to come with me, or…?"

Drew growled in the affirmative, and I made sure to include him in the transportation spell I used to travel back to the inn.

Jia joined me a heartbeat later, peering through the window. "Why is Jennifer in there?"

"Good question." I guessed my transportation spell had sent her here and not to the witches' headquarters.

We entered the lobby, where Jennifer had slumped in a chair that Allie must have fetched from the restaurant. Since Drew was still in werewolf form, he didn't enter the inn but waited outside, his shaggy form curled up in front of the doors.

"What's he doing, playing security guard?" I barely had time to blink before Carey ran over and hugged me so tight that I could have sworn she'd cracked a rib or two. "Ow. I'm okay."

"Maura!" she said. "Did Mina hurt you?"

"I'm not the one who's hurt." I raised my voice to address

Allie, who'd come out of the games room at the back. "We left Shelton fighting her."

"Come on, sit down in here." Allie beckoned us into the games room, which was currently occupied by the ghosts.

Jia helped Jennifer stagger over to the sofa, while I sank into an armchair.

Allie ran out of the room, saying over her shoulder, "I'll get a potion brewing for both of you. Carey, can you help with the guests?"

"I'm fine," I told Carey when she shot me a look of concern. "You help your mother."

Soon enough, Allie returned carrying several mugs of some kind of potion, one of which she gave to me. It tasted somewhere between a fruit cocktail and hot soup, which was a hell of a weird combination, but it made me feel marginally less unsteady on my feet.

Drew entered as I was finishing off the mug, dressed in rumpled clothes that he must have acquired from somewhere after he'd turned back into a human. "Maura—I've called the office to send some people to watch the inn, but it's not going to be Mina's only target, is it?"

"It'll certainly be her first one." I rested my head against the back of the chair and closed my eyes. "Harold has her talisman, but that might not matter anymore. The demon..."

"Do you know whereabouts her hideout actually is?" he asked. "If we have her location, I can send more people to surround her."

"No. I don't know where it is." A wave of defeat washed over me. "It was an ordinary house. Might've been anywhere. I can use a transportation spell to have a closer look, but if I were her, I'd leave as soon as I'd finished—" *With Shelton*, I finished silently.

"Don't." He leaned closer, his forehead brushing mine.

"Don't blame yourself. Shelton knew what he was getting into."

"I know." I glimpsed Jennifer watching me from the sofa. "Jennifer, do *you* know where Mina's hideout is?"

"No," she mumbled. "She took me in there blindfolded. And the room had no windows."

"You must have seen something."

Everyone turned expectantly to Jennifer. The potion had restored a little colour to her pale face, but exhaustion lined her features, and her usually impeccable blond hair hung lankly on either side of her head.

"If you want me to tell you her plans, I don't know what they are," Jennifer said wearily. "She shut me in a room and fed my life force to her demon once a day."

"I thought demons needed to kill frequently to survive." I racked my mind to remember my training. "That's why people don't make a habit of summoning them on a whim unless they don't care how many bodies they leave behind. Including their own, come to that."

Jennifer shuddered. "No… instead of feeding me to her demon in one go, she let it siphon off my life force a bit at a time."

"Ouch." I hadn't known it was possible to sustain a demon in that manner, but I freely admitted to not being an expert on the subject. "When exactly did she summon the demon?"

"A few days ago," she replied. "Before that, she left me alone most of the time. I thought she planned to use me as a… a sacrifice, but…"

"But she didn't kill you." Strange. "She must have found some other poor soul to sacrifice instead."

Once she'd had the book. *The book.* After everything I'd been through to protect it, it'd ended up back in her hands.

"It was my assumption that she realised that capturing

locals to feed to the demon would draw too much attention," she mumbled. "I never asked."

I sat bolt upright when darkness filled the room, but it was just Harold the Reaper. When Xavier appeared, too, the ghosts all scattered with shrieks of alarm at the sight of his scythe.

I slumped in my seat again. "I thought you were staying at home."

"I wish *you* had," Harold countered. "Now you've made the whole situation worse."

"Me?" I said indignantly. "I'm not the maniac who summoned a demon and let it possess her on purpose."

"She summoned *what?*" Xavier said, aghast. "You didn't mention that."

"You were banishing her monsters at the time." I rubbed my forehead. "Yeah, she already summoned a demon, and she's been feeding Jennifer's life force to it for the past week."

"Now we're in trouble," Harold growled. "A demon… she doesn't need to wait until Samhain to claim power."

"What makes you think one demon will be enough for her?" If she'd achieved her goals, she'd have come after me already. No… I had the sinking suspicion that the demon was simply the opening act.

"I'd wager you're right." Xavier sounded unusually defeated. "I have to tell my boss."

"Now?" I asked, alarmed. "Mina might attack us at any instant."

"I can't fight a demon without telling my boss," Xavier said. "It's far beyond my orders."

Harold scoffed. "Apprentices."

"If you'd been there, we might have had a fighting chance," I shot at him. "If Shelton dies… what then?"

"What then?" he echoed. "We protect our own."

He strode out of the room without another word. Xavier gave us one last apologetic look and then followed him.

Jennifer rose shakily to her feet. "I have to return to my coven."

"No." Allie appeared in the doorway. "You can stay here as long as you need to recover."

Jennifer straightened upright, holding onto the back of the sofa for balance. "I wouldn't be much of a coven leader if I hid here when my fellow witches need me."

*Do they need you?* "They never bothered coming to save you from Mina."

"Nevertheless." She walked to the door on shaky legs.

Allie stepped aside, visibly reluctant, as the coven leader left the games room.

I rose to my feet, too, but Drew caught my arm. "Maura, you need rest."

Helpless anger seized me. "Someone has to act, and it's definitely not going to be Harold. Or the witches."

"So?" Mart came drifting over, looking somewhat more recovered than I felt. "I don't want to die either, Maura. It's not just your life at stake."

The other ghosts gathered around him. Little Vicky peered up at me, her eyes bright with anxiety, and the others wore similar expressions. Even with the Reapers gone, the sense of helplessness in the air was tangible.

My hands fisted. No. I refused to give up that easily.

"Maura, say the word, and I'll help you," said Allie. "What do you need?"

Both the ghosts and the living alike watched me, waiting for me to give instructions.

I lifted my head and spoke. "We're going to Mina-proof Hawkwood Hollow."

## 10

Mina-proofing the inn mostly consisted of Allie, Carey, and Jia setting up shielding spells on the walls and on the area around the river. I helped as much as I could, but fighting Mina had taken more out of me than I wanted to admit. Eventually, Drew ordered me to go to bed.

I slept hard and woke up in a panic, convinced I'd slept through Mina's arrival.

"Relax," Mart said when I jumped out of bed. "Allie covered the inn with enough alarm spells that half the town would be alerted if Mina did show up."

"Can half the town beat a demon?"

"Yes, actually," said Mart. "There's a reason Mina locked herself up in a room nobody could get into or out of. Faced with the town's entire population, she'd find herself ripped apart from that demon sooner or later."

"But Shelton had to face her alone." A renewed pang of guilt hit me.

Mart threw a pillow at my head. "Stop that," he ordered.

"I'll not have any of your moping. We have an evil witch to defeat."

Yeah. We were down to four days until Halloween, and Mina would be back for revenge soon enough.

I shooed Mart out of the room so I could properly shower and generally put myself back together after my fight with Mina. Drew had left a message on my phone saying that he'd been called into the office to give a report as to what exactly had gone on in the field yesterday, but he promised to drop by later so we could discuss what to do next.

Downstairs, Mart and I found Allie pacing around the lobby. She looked as though she hadn't slept a wink. "Oh… hello, Maura."

"Hey, I didn't tell you to stay up all night putting up protective spells," I protested.

"I had to convince Jia to go home eventually," she said. "And I wasn't going to make Carey stay up all night. I'm fine. Our safety is more important."

"My safety." I grimaced. "This is my fault. If I hadn't baited Mina…"

"No, I should have set up defensive spells sooner," she said distractedly. "I was fixated on making Halloween normal for Carey."

"I still painted a target on our backs," I admitted. "I didn't have a plan. We got Jennifer back, but Mina is more powerful than ever."

She wasn't alone either. If she and the demon were working hand in hand, who knew how the situation might escalate before Halloween?

"Oh, there's Carey." Allie waved at her daughter, who'd entered the lobby with an anxious expression.

"Maura." Carey ran to me. "Are you all right?"

"I'm fine," I told her. "There's not much that can't be fixed with a good night's sleep."

"Good." She bounded through the automatic doors into the restaurant, and I felt a renewed surge of admiration for Allie's ability to keep it together while all hell was breaking loose.

As I was piling my plate at the breakfast buffet table, I noticed a distinct lack of any ghosts in the restaurant. "Mart... where are the other ghosts?"

"Hiding in the games room," he replied. "All the more food for me."

I snatched my plate out of his reach. "I don't want you making my breakfast freeze. Go talk to the other ghosts instead."

The guests didn't appear to have noticed anything was wrong, but it'd been dark outside when Allie had been running around putting up defensive spells the previous day, and the inn itself didn't *look* any different. Especially on the inside, where Carey's decorations covered every inch of the walls and ceiling. That included the glowing banner that reminded me of how few days we had left before the night when Mina would have access to even more power than she had already.

Drew showed up at midmorning, looking as sleepless as Allie did. Jia took over serving customers so that I could get some peace to talk to him.

I ran over to Drew, and he hugged me. "You look better than you did yesterday."

"Great backhanded compliment there," Mart said from across the room.

"I'm fine," I told Drew, ignoring my brother. "How's the team? I should have asked if they were okay after fighting those monsters yesterday."

"They're fine," he replied. "Physically, I mean. I get the impression that not all of them will step forward the next time I ask for volunteers to help fight Mina."

I winced. "Figures. Did you mention our plans to set up defences around the rest of the town?"

"I did," he confirmed. "I've sent a few wizards to cover the boundaries of the town with defensive spells, and I told them to put sage down too."

"You're learning." I shot him a smile. "Sage can even keep out a demon, but I wouldn't put it past Mina to try to find a way around it."

"Exactly," said Drew. "There have been a few arguments, especially about the tunnels."

*The tunnels.* I pressed a hand to my forehead. "Of course. I'm guessing collapsing them will cause issues?"

"That's what we're trying to determine," he said. "They run underneath the river, and given the history of the floods…"

"Yeah, we don't want to make Mina's job even easier," I said. "You can close them off, right?"

"Yes, but we'd need the coven's permission."

Typical. "If you mean Jennifer, I'm sure she'll say yes, won't she?"

"I think it's safe to say some other coven members will object," he said. "I haven't spoken to Jennifer since she returned to work."

"Yeah… we should probably check up on her," I said. "If I were her, I'd be asking questions about her fellow coven members' loyalties."

"She declined my offer to send some of my team back with her last night to watch out for trouble," he said. "She's as stubborn as ever despite her ordeal."

"The others should be grovelling to her after they didn't even try to help her escape from Mina," I said. "You know, I think we should pay her a visit. I'll see if Jia can cover for me for an hour or so."

Once I'd let Jia and Allie know where I was going, Drew

and I left the inn and crossed the bridge over the river. While the town didn't *look* any different, the strong smell of sage permeated the air, and there was a noticeable lack of ghosts lingering on street corners and roaming around buildings.

"Weird," I muttered. "The ghosts at the inn were hiding too."

"Were they?" asked Drew.

"Yeah. I guess the sage scared them off," I said. "I guess we can check in with old Harold and see what he has to say for himself."

*Shelton.* A fresh wave of guilt hit me. Harold hadn't offered to help his fellow Reaper fight Mina, and *he* hadn't been sucker-punched by a demon, so I pushed my guilt towards him instead. There was Xavier, too, though he'd been limited in what his boss would allow him to do. I didn't know if the Grim Reaper had let him come back up north yet, but if he didn't, we'd be down yet another Reaper ally. Unless I talked to my dad again.

*Oh, he'll be thrilled that Mina already summoned a demon.*

When Drew and I reached the coven headquarters, I glimpsed a few people downstairs in the lobby. The doors slid open, revealing none other than Priscilla.

"You!" I pointed at her. "I hope you're apologising to your coven leader for failing to show up and help us rescue her from Mina."

"She's not my coven leader," Priscilla said without a hint of remorse. "And I was outvoted in the end. The others decided not to trust a Reaper to keep us safe."

"Safe?" I bit back a laugh. "There's nothing safe about fighting against someone like Mina. Any witches who volunteered to help should have known they were risking their lives. The police didn't have a problem with going along with my plan."

"It wasn't your plan. It was your Reaper friends'."

"Shelton risked his life to help Jennifer and me get out in one piece," I retaliated, acutely aware of the other witches goggling at us from across the lobby. These included Wendy, who stood at the foot of the wide staircase and wrung her hands in her usual agitated manner.

"It's done now," Priscilla said.

"No, it isn't," I countered. "Mina's still out there and angrier than ever. Jennifer doesn't need you coming here and rubbing it in her face."

Priscilla narrowed her eyes at me. "I came here to give information to the coven leader, actually, but I don't think you deserve to hear it."

She stalked past Drew and me, through the doors, and out into the gloomy street. Out of the corner of my eye, I spied Wendy trying to surreptitiously slip back upstairs without anyone noticing.

"You're welcome for rescuing your leader," I said to her. "Where is she? Upstairs?"

Without waiting for an answer, I began climbing the staircase. Wendy gave me a frightened look and scuttled ahead of me while Drew caught up to me. At the top of the stairs, I rapped on the door to Jennifer's office.

"Enter," she called.

I did so. Jennifer sat at her desk as if she'd never been gone. She'd restyled her hair and cleaned herself up and generally looked far more put together than the previous day.

Wendy inched into the room behind me, eyeing her coven leader as if she was a bomb about to go off.

"Maura," said Jennifer. "Drew. To what to I owe the pleasure?"

*Is she seriously pretending the past few weeks never happened?* "Have you spoken to your coven yet?"

"Of course I have."

"And…" I sought a diplomatic way of phrasing the question and drew a blank. "Did any of them offer an apology for not coming to your rescue?"

"Really, Maura," she said. "If I condemned everyone who didn't come to help me escape Mina's captivity, I'd have no coven members left."

Wendy let out a faint moan. I ignored her. "Aren't you worried some of them might be working with Mina?"

"No," she replied tersely. "I am not. Is that all you wanted to ask me, Maura? You might gather that I have a large amount of paperwork to catch up with."

"Paperwork." I gave a disbelieving laugh. "Mina's going to attack the town on Halloween—or before if she's still furious enough with me to come here for a shot at revenge. She's possessed by a *demon*. Does the coven know that?"

"Don't talk so loudly." She caught Wendy's eye for an instant; the other witch had paled to the colour of sour milk but didn't otherwise act surprised, which indicated that the coven leader had confided in her assistant, at least. "I had no desire to cause a panic."

"I think Mina showing up with her demon in tow would be a cause for panic, don't you?"

"I agree," Drew said, stepping up to my side. "We must accept the real possibility of Mina launching an attack on Hawkwood Hollow at any instant. My team have been setting up defensive barriers around the entire town, but there's one weak spot: the tunnels."

"You want to close off the tunnels?" Jennifer asked. "I thought you needed them as proof of Mina's crimes."

"They're illegal sources of dark magic that she might use for the same purpose again," I said. "Besides, we don't need them to provide proof when we have your testimony that Mina tried to torture you and fed your soul to her pet demon for weeks. I'm pretty sure that's more than enough to have her put away for life."

Jennifer shook her head firmly. "The rest of the coven will never agree to close the tunnels."

"You decided not to tell them that Mina's possessed by a demon," I reminded her. "I think you can skip a vote on this one too."

Her shoulders slumped. "Fine. If you want to deal with the other witches' complaints, Drew, on your own head be it."

"I'll take the risk," Drew said. "This is a situation that merits urgent action, however unpopular those decisions might be."

Jennifer made a sceptical noise. "You might be reacting too late. Mina has no need of the tunnels to enact any plan of hers now."

"Maybe, but we don't need to leave open an easy route of access to the town," I replied. "Are you sure she didn't give anything away while you were her captive?"

"I already told you everything," she said. "Mina's not in the habit of conversing with her prisoners."

"Did you tell Priscilla too?" I queried. "I take it she offered an apology. She was supposed to come with us to help rescue you, but she never showed up."

"Priscilla doesn't owe me loyalty," she said. "As a matter of fact, she offered to trade information on safe houses in the event that we have to evacuate."

"That's why she came here?" I stared at her. "*That's* your plan if Mina attacks Hawkwood Hollow? You intend to run away?"

"Sometimes, that's the option that results in the fewest deaths," she said. "I won't pretend any of us has a chance against Mina, especially not with her new demonic ally."

"Unbelievable." I turned to Drew. "Well, *I'm* not giving up that easily. Right, Drew?"

"Right." He addressed Jennifer again. "Thank you for cooperating. I'll let you know when we've finished sealing off the tunnels."

Jennifer gave no reply. Neither did Wendy, though she watched wide-eyed while she scuttled away from the door.

Drew and I left Jennifer's office and descended the stairs into the lobby. Nobody else was around, including Priscilla, and I couldn't help wondering if the other witches had figured out what was going on. I'd have thought some would be glad of their leader's return, but if they were, they hadn't shown their faces.

When we left, Drew veered towards the police station, but my own attention went towards the cemetery.

"You want to talk to Harold?" he guessed.

"I don't *want* to, but he needs to answer for ditching Shelton and leaving him to fight Mina alone."

Also, I was kind of concerned at the absence of the ghosts. They couldn't have left the town altogether, but they'd picked a fine time to go into hiding.

"All right." Drew gave me a brief kiss. "I'll see you later. Hopefully, we can get those tunnels dealt with by the morning's end."

*Me too.* In the meantime, I made for the cemetery gates. To my surprise, I found Mart hovering outside the Reaper's cottage.

"I got bored at the inn" was his explanation. "Nobody's around?"

"Where are the other ghosts?" I asked. "Are they all hiding?"

"Must be." He glowered at the closed door to Harold's cottage. "Him too. He won't answer the door."

"He'd better answer to *me*." I stepped closer to the small

cottage, which bore the number 42 above the door for reasons I still had yet to figure out. "I doubt he'll volunteer to help Drew's team seal off the tunnels, mind."

"The coven leader actually said yes?"

"Yeah, but she also said that if Mina shows up, she'll run out of town and go into hiding, same as Priscilla did."

Mart sent a rude gesture in the general direction of the coven headquarters. "Want me to talk some sense into her?"

"Nah, I think she's beyond that. Save it for Harold."

"And if *he* doesn't see sense?"

"Then I'll go talk to Dad again," I decided. "He needs to know that Mina summoned a demon. If that doesn't convince him to defy the Council and come help… I don't know what will."

## 11

Harold didn't answer the door at first, but I persisted and knocked again. And again. Finally, the door swung open.

"What?" he snapped. "If you're here to ask permission to borrow my scythe for your suicidal rescue mission—"

"What rescue mission?" I frowned. "I don't follow."

"Really?" Harold grunted. "I thought you were determined to throw yourself into Mina's path to save your fellow Reaper."

"You think Shelton's *alive?*" I said disbelievingly. "I thought... I thought for sure that she'd have killed him. Besides, you're the one who was adamant that leaving him behind was what he would have wanted us to do."

"Obviously," he said. "She killed the other Reaper for the book, but Shelton is a potential source of information on her enemies. For that reason, she's likely to have spared his life for the time being."

I had my doubts. "The demon can't feed on him, given that Reapers are immune. What other reason would she have to keep him around?"

"You think I know?" he said. "You're asking me to understand the mind of a witch who willingly made a contract with a demon."

"Yes, and she must have been pretty convincing for the demon not to have killed her outright," I added. "Anyway, I came here to let you know that we're Mina-proofing the town and ask if you wanted to help, but I'm guessing the answer is no."

"What do you possibly need me to do?" he scoffed. "Unless you want to get rid of the ghosts, you have little need for a Reaper."

"Where *are* the ghosts?"

"There's one right behind you."

"Very funny." I glanced at Mart, who looked equally unimpressed. "The ghosts have gone into hiding for a reason."

"Yes, they have," he retorted. "Namely, because someone decided to douse the entire town in sage."

"The inn was already covered in sage, and they didn't seem to mind then." I shook my head at him. "You should know that the police are filling in the tunnels."

"Several years too late."

Honestly. The guy was more efficient at raining on my parade than a monsoon. "Fine. I'm going to talk to my dad."

He closed the door in my face in midsentence. I held out my arm to stop Mart from floating through the wooden surface.

"Do you think he's right?" I asked my brother as I closed the cemetery gate behind us. "Would Mina have let Shelton live?"

"You're asking the wrong person," he said. "I'd say no. She's a mass murderer with a god complex who doesn't want the Reapers interfering in her plans."

*Yeah, he's right on that one.*

"And… do you think we should speak to Dad again?"

"Only if you want Mum to show up on the doorstep, wailing about being neglected."

"I can't involve her in this." The situation was already spiralling out of control, and the last thing I needed to do was to paint a target on Greenwood Lake as large as the one floating above Hawkwood Hollow.

"I never said it was a good idea to drag her into our mess," Mart said. "That's why we're better off placating her before she shows up at the inn."

"Might be a bit late for that, given that I've been ignoring her messages all week." How on earth was I supposed to respond to her entreaties that I give her a blow-by-blow update on how my week was going? *Well, yesterday, I had the bright idea of letting my Reaper ally track down Mina and summoned her monsters on top of us then accidentally transported myself into her hideout and really ticked her off in the process.*

I went back to the inn first to let the others know the plan and to send a message to Dad ahead of time. I didn't *think* my mother had gone so far as to spy on his text messages, but if she had, I'd just have to risk it. Once I'd warned him of our upcoming arrival, Mart and I set off for our dad's house.

Jia had offered to come with me, but I knew my dad wouldn't talk in front of any non-Reapers. Besides, someone had to stay and keep an eye out for trouble. I knew I was tempting fate by leaving at a time of crisis myself, but if I convinced Dad to come back with me, it'd be worth the risk.

One trip through the afterworld later, Mart and I landed outside the Reaper's house in Greenwood Lake. I walked to the door and knocked, hoping the coven's spies had taken the day off.

Dad answered the door with his usual long-suffering expression, and Mart zipped into the house ahead of me. I entered the living room, this time standing instead of sitting in one of the uncomfortable chairs.

"You might have gathered that Shelton's plan didn't go as he intended," I began.

"Yes," he replied. "Are you going to explain why I can't find him?"

"You can't find him?" My heart plunged. "Harold hasn't told you yet?"

"Told me what?"

"Mina summoned a demon and let it possess her."

His lips parted. If he had been anyone other than my dad, I'd have taken his reaction as nothing but mild surprise rather than shock. "Are you sure?"

"Of course I'm sure," I said. "She was feeding Jennifer's life force to the demon rather than drawing attention by dragging human victims into her hideout. Shelton used some kind of tracking spell to find her, but even he didn't expect her to already be possessed. He pretty much forced me to take Jennifer and run, leaving him to fight her alone."

Dad made a noise of irritation. "Let me guess: You tried to fight her anyway?"

I dropped my gaze. "I'm not happy at having left him behind, if that's what you mean. Harold suggested that she might have kept him alive, but if you can't sense him…"

"He's not likely to survive in her captivity for long," Dad said. "She already killed one Reaper, and given her anti-Reaper defences, she had an edge."

"If you haven't heard from Harold, you won't know that I stole her talisman." I let a hint of satisfaction creep into my voice. "With Shelton's help. She was wearing a ring that made her Reaper-proof."

"That's something," he said. "I sincerely hope Harold intends to hand that ring over to the authorities."

"When he did the same with that book, she just stole it

back," I reminded him. "And without Shelton, we're down one Reaper ally even if Xavier comes back."

"Who's Xavier?"

"Reaper apprentice from Ivory Beach," I replied. "He came to help at Shelton's request since you didn't answer his calls."

"I've been trying to keep the Reaper Council from coming after you," he said. "They've been poking around, asking questions."

*Dammit.* "You mean they're investigating Mina?"

"Yes," he said. "They asked which coven she came from. I couldn't lie."

"You told them about Hawkwood Hollow?" My hands curled into fists. "You do realise Mina might attack at any moment? I won't have my home turn into a battleground."

"I also told them she wasn't currently there," he said. "That said, it's the obvious place to start looking."

"You know that won't help anyone," I said. "They'll get fixated on the ghosts and forget all about her."

"Do you have a better idea?" he challenged.

"I don't know." I paced across the room in frustration. "I also don't know why she hasn't come after me for revenge yet, unless Shelton distracted her. I'm sure she still plans to do *something* on Halloween, but I mean, what's worse than a demon?"

"If I were you, I wouldn't ask that question," Dad growled. "I've yet to discern how she killed that Reaper, but I have an inkling he was the sacrifice for her to summon her demon."

"No wonder it's so powerful." Chills raced down my spine. "At least Hawkwood Hollow isn't going to be as attractive a target after the police finish filling in the tunnels so she can't use them for any future rituals."

"That doesn't matter," he said. "Your entire town sits on top of a nexus point held together with little more than one Reaper's willpower. If she tries another ritual on Samhain, it'll crack the gates wide-open. Aside from whatever monstrosities she might unleash, it'll be a catastrophe for the people of Hawkwood Hollow, including the dead."

"Including me?" Mart asked, his voice quieter than usual.

"No." I raised my own voice sharply. "No way. I'll stop her first."

"If she's already possessed, it'll be difficult," Dad said. "If not impossible."

"Harold already told me as much, but the people who keep telling me I can't do it aren't making much of an effort to do anything themselves," I shot at him. "Filling in the tunnels will slow her down."

"Demons don't feel threatened by physical boundaries," he said. "If you *really* want to keep her out, you'll have to put a full-strength barrier around the town itself, which is bound to irritate some of your ghosts."

"I don't know. They don't seem to mind the sage at the inn." I looked at Mart, but he was peering out the window with an apparently indifferent air. "They trust me."

I refused to use the phrase "Ghost Protector" in front of my dad, but he sighed anyway. "Your commitment to those ghosts is going to get you killed."

"Mina is the one who killed them," I said. "It's not like they can leave of their own accord. Besides, I'm committed to protecting the living *and* the dead."

"I won't argue with you." A touch of weariness entered his voice. "If you want to keep both Mina *and* the Council away, the only option is to find her first."

"What—go back to Mina's hideout?"

"You know the way, don't you?"

"Yes." I frowned. "You *want* me to risk my life by going back? After Shelton sacrificed himself so that Jennifer and I could escape?"

"There's a good chance she's changed locations by now,"

Dad said. "If not, she won't be expecting you to come back. Besides, I'll be with you."

"You… you will?" What had changed his mind? Maybe he wanted to help Shelton after all, but I had an inkling that Mina would have ensured we couldn't take her by surprise again.

"Yes." He indicated the door. "Well?"

*What's he up to?* "Will you be able to sense her location now that she isn't wearing her Reaper-proof ring?"

"That's the intention, yes."

Weird. Maybe Shelton's sacrifice had caused my dad to have a change of heart where Mina was concerned, though it was a lot easier for us to take her on without her wearing a Reaper-proof talisman. Even if she was still possessed by a demon.

I checked my pockets even though I'd taken to carrying sage everywhere, along with my wand, for weeks now. No scythe, but it couldn't be helped. "All right. Mart, are you coming?"

My brother had drifted over to the back window, where he made a great show of peering outside. "No."

"What do you mean no?"

"The coven is already watching you," he said. "Besides, I bet she's not there."

*Are the coven members seriously spying on my dad's house?* "Mum's not outside, is she?"

"Not yet." He swivelled towards me. "I think someone needs to distract them."

"If you're volunteering…" I paused. "What do you want in exchange this time? I already bought you those Halloween lights."

"A racing car."

"What?" I yelped. "That's impossible in a dozen ways."

"A broomstick, then."

"You do realise you can already fly?"

I heard a faint laugh, but when I looked at my dad, he wore a determinedly serious expression. Well, well. My brother had worked his charm on him at last. He wore everyone down eventually, and it was no wonder he'd had an easier time placating Mum than I had.

"Okay… how about I promise to visit Mum on a regular basis, starting from the weekend after we get rid of Mina?"

"Only if you promise not to let yourself get killed just to get off the hook."

"Not happening." The notion of spending more time than necessary at Mum's house filled me with a horror that was quite distinct from the idea of meeting my death at Mina's hands, but maybe it was time to stop running away. That was Mina's thing and now Jennifer's too. Not mine.

Dad and I entered the afterworld, and I pictured the house where Mina had been hiding. As the darkness cleared, I stepped out into the spot where Jennifer and I had made our escape. The door stood ajar, revealing a hallway carpeted in grey and wallpapered in beige. Rather bland… and now, as I scanned my surroundings and spied a few other houses spread out on either side, a sense of familiarity pinged in my awareness.

"This is… I know this place. Isn't it a normal town?"

"It's the town next door to Greenwood Lake." Dad glided over to the doors. "She's not here. Nobody is."

"She's found a new hideout." A measure of relief and anger rose inside my chest. "I guess it was inevitable after we crashed her party yesterday."

Without replying, Dad paced ahead of me into the hallway.

"What are you doing, looking for Shelton?" I followed, my skin crawling at the thought of how Jennifer had been imprisoned in here for weeks. "She won't have left him behind."

"No." Dad halted. "No. When a Reaper dies, no traces are left behind."

"Wouldn't you have sensed him die?" I would have, too, assuming they'd been within the vicinity of both of us. If not… there was no telling *where* they'd gone.

Dad began to walk upstairs. "Dark magic was used in this house."

"You don't say." I trod on the lowest step. "Jennifer was imprisoned in one of the rooms up there, but we didn't have the chance to check the others."

Dad continued to walk until he reached the landing. I stuck close behind him, my own Reaper senses detecting a faint chill in the air but nothing else. I didn't sense any living creatures, human or otherwise, within the house's boundaries. No ghosts either.

I caught up to Dad as he faced one of the rooms off the landing, darkness curling above his palms. My heart jumped, recognising the room where Shelton and I had fought Mina, but no traces of either of them remained inside. He backed out of the room and tried the next one then the next.

At the last room on the landing, the strong smell of herbs permeated the air when he opened the door. Part of the carpet had been pulled up, and my gaze instantly went to the chalk marks that had been scratched onto the bare floorboards in a circular pattern.

"She used a ritual in here," I said. "Is this where she summoned the demon?"

"I think she summoned more than that." Dad pointed at the chalk marks, within which I spied several ominous stains, dark against the pale floorboards. "More than one sacrifice was made."

"Who?" My skin crawled. "Not… that Reaper?"

"There's a strong possibility," Dad growled. "That said, she almost certainly killed several humans here."

"Lovely." No wonder she hadn't wanted to draw even more attention by capturing people to feed to the demon afterwards. "What's she planning to do on Halloween, then?"

Dad didn't answer. He turned back to me, his expression unusually tense. "What did she say? When you fought her."

"She said I'm not a strong-enough Reaper." My voice wavered despite my best efforts. "Even if my powers had been working, I don't know that I could have beaten her. Hell, I wouldn't have even been able to find her without Shelton's help."

"You would if you knew how," he said. "There's no difference between you and me except a few hundred years of training."

"A few hundred years." I bit back a laugh, averting my eyes from the creepy stains on the floor. "I can't learn all that in a few days."

"Can't you?"

My phone buzzed, cutting off my answer. At first, I thought it was Mum calling to take me to task for visiting town without dropping by at her house. Then I recognised Jia's number. Ignoring Dad's disgruntled sigh, I tapped on the call.

"Maura!" Jia gasped into the phone. "We need your help."

A fizzling noise cut off my reply, leaving silence behind.

## 12

"Jia." I lowered my phone, my heart racing. "Sorry, Dad. See you later?"

I didn't hesitate long enough to hear his arguments. I raised my wand and cast a transportation spell to head back to Hawkwood Hollow.

My feet touched down in the inn's lobby. I looked wildly around, but nothing appeared to be out of place. Where was Jia?

As I took a step towards the adjoining doors to the restaurant, they slid open, and Allie came hurrying over to me. "Maura?"

"Where's Jia, do you know?" I pulled out my phone again. "What's going on?"

"Something to do with the coven," said Allie anxiously. "Jia went to find out more."

*The coven.* In a flick of my wand, I used another transportation spell to travel to the high street, where I launched into a run towards the coven headquarters.

A commotion had erupted inside. Spells flew left and right across the lobby, and it took a moment for me to spot Jia duelling another witch. *Priscilla.* Around them, several police officers stood stock-still as though hit with freeze-frame spells, while Jennifer stood back against the wall with two other witches advancing on her. Both were people I recognised as Priscilla's allies, including the pink-hatted witch who'd treated me with such disdain at the coven meeting.

"Hey!" I shouted. "What do you think you're doing?" Enacting a coup, I guessed.

Running into the lobby, I fired off a freezing charm of my own, but one of the witches spun around and cast a counter-spell. Both spells fizzled out, and Jennifer sank to the ground. At a guess, she still hadn't recovered from her ordeal over the past few weeks, and instead of helping, Priscilla and her allies had intentionally taken advantage of her weakness.

I freed the police officers from the immobilising spells first and then called on my Reaper powers. It might have been cheating, but the look on the pink-hatted witch's face when I used the shadows to knock her wand flying out of her hand was priceless. I did the same to her ally while Jia got the upper hand on Priscilla and used a spell that knocked her off her feet.

"Thought you could overthrow your leader, did you?" I flicked my own wand, sending the other two witches toppling into a heap. "I knew you weren't trustworthy, but this is a new low for you, Priscilla."

"This isn't what you think," Priscilla said.

"I'll be the judge of that," Drew said from behind me. "You're all under arrest."

The other officers moved at his command, and within minutes, they had the other witches restrained and in handcuffs. Priscilla resignedly put her hands up to let Drew cuff her too.

While the police hauled the conspirators away, I moved

towards Jennifer. She'd struggled upright, but she was still pale and shaky, and Wendy was nowhere in sight.

"What was that?" I asked Jennifer. "Was she trying to depose you?"

"I was trying to save the coven," Priscilla called from the doorway. "From Mina."

"That's enough." Drew nudged her through the door. "Come on."

"Wait." Leaving Jennifer, I ran after Drew and addressed his captive. "Tell me what you were really doing. You planned to bring her back, didn't you?"

"No," said Priscilla, sounding insulted. "She—Mina—she drove us out of our hideout. We didn't have any choice but to come back here."

"She drove you out?" *That's where she went?* Of all the places Mina might have gone, the other witches' hideout hadn't even occurred to me. "So you decided to do the same to Jennifer, did you?"

"Come on." Drew urged her down the street, following his fellow officers over the road towards the jail.

"Mina drove them out of their hideout?" Jia ran to my side, staring after the conspirators. "Is that where she is?"

"It'd explain why we didn't find her in her own hideout."

Jia's jaw dropped. "You went *there*? Please tell me you didn't go alone."

"I'll explain later." I glanced over my shoulder at the lobby. As Jennifer shuffled towards the stairs, Wendy came running into view, wringing her hands as usual.

"Are they gone?" she asked.

"Yes, no thanks to you," I said. "Some assistant you are."

Wendy wilted like a water-starved plant. "I called the police. I couldn't get enough coven members together to help."

"Figures." I left her with the beleaguered coven leader and followed Jia across the road towards the police station.

"I thought you were visiting your dad," Jia said to me. "How on earth did you end up in Mina's house?"

"His idea, not mine, believe it or not," I said. "We went to check out her base, but she'd taken off. Then you called..."

"Why'd Mina invade Priscilla's safe house?" Jia wrinkled her nose. "Weird. Not really the best way to avoid detection."

"I'm not sure she *wants* to avoid being found at this point," I said. "None of her decisions make much sense. I guess if the demon's at the wheel, it doesn't necessarily matter."

"She might have *wanted* those other witches to come running back to cause chaos here," Jia suggested. "That'd play into her hands."

"True." I halted outside the police station and watched Drew directing his officers to take Priscilla and her allies to the holding cells. "I'm going to see if I can get any more clues out of her."

"You sure?" Jia's gaze went back to the coven headquarters. "All right. I'll head back to the inn."

"See you in a bit." I checked my phone—no messages from Dad, but Mum had sent five asking me to come join her and Mart in reminiscing about old times. Hoping he could keep her distracted a bit longer, I entered the police station and walked over to Drew.

"You have good timing," he told me. "Priscilla is still claiming that Mina moved in on her safe house. I find it hard to believe, I admit."

"Dad and I found her own safe house abandoned." I lowered my voice when I spied Petra peering out of one of the rooms. "Have you heard anything from her allies?"

"What, the ones in the jail?" He shook his head. "I heard of some restless behaviour in there last night but no attempted breakouts. They're under high security."

"I know, but something's afoot with her."

I gave Petra a stony look, and she slipped out of the room, not remotely ashamed to have been caught eavesdropping.

"I wonder if her friends know what her game is?"

I doubted that they knew she'd *already* been possessed by a demon, but I'd been so fixated on preventing Mina from breaking into the town that I'd momentarily forgotten the allies who were incarcerated inside Hawkwood Hollow itself.

"They might," he said doubtfully. "We can't move them to another jail without risking another attempted escape."

*That's what I was afraid of.* The trouble was that Hawkwood Hollow was small enough that its security measures had nothing on the bigger magical jails, and there was a limit to what the police force could do when it came to dealing with enemies in multiple places at once. "Can I have a word with them?"

"Now?" He glanced over at the jail door. "All right."

Petra watched with disapproval as I followed Drew through the door and past the holding cells in which Priscilla and her allies had been ensconced. Through another door lay the most secure area of the jail, where Mina's allies were incarcerated, including the former librarian, Debora Lowe, and Angela and Maria, who'd once been prominent coven members.

Debora was the first to spot me, and when she did, she put down the book she'd been reading and smirked. "I knew you'd come here after you failed to catch Mina."

"Actually, we did get the coven leader out of her clutches," I said.

"She's no coven leader."

I'd expected a similar response, and I addressed mine to everyone in the surrounding cells. "Were you involved in that coup, by any chance?"

Several laughs answered, and Debora gave a bland smile. "Do I look as if I'm involved in anything?"

"Yes, actually," I said. "It's pretty much a given that if Mina's scheming, so are you. Planning another breakout?"

"Would I admit it if I was?"

"You might." I moved closer to her cell. "We both know she plans to act on Halloween, if not beforehand. What's the next step beyond summoning a demon?"

I'd hoped to shock her into admitting she knew her leader less well than she'd thought, but she merely laughed. "You should know, being a Reaper."

"I'm a Reaper, not a demonic contractor and a mass murderer," I corrected. "You know some of how her mind works. Why would she summon a demon and let it possess her at the risk of her own life?"

"Why wouldn't she?" Debora asked. "That was always her plan. A demon running amok is dangerous. Chained to a person, it's controlled."

"It's not chained to her, though. She wouldn't share power with another person."

"You'd be surprised," said the witch. "You might have trouble believing it, but she's trying to look out for all our interests. She never wanted to make an enemy of you."

"No, only to cover up murders and other crimes." I was done with her making excuses for her former coven leader. "You know, if I had my way, I'd incarcerate the lot of you in the afterworld instead and let the monsters eat you."

"You're all talk."

"I'm really not." Some of my frustration leaked out, and as I lifted my hands, the afterworld responded with a deeper chill than I expected, as though I'd plunged my fist into an icy ocean.

"What are you doing?" Alarm flickered across Debora's face.

"Nothing." I dropped my hands, but the darkness didn't go away. The temperature plummeted, sending my Reaper senses into overdrive.

"What—?" I spun around to face a wide-eyed Drew.

"Maura, what's going on?"

"I don't know—" I cut off in a gasp as a flurry of bright figures appeared, shining against the darkness.

Ghosts. Everywhere. They swarmed through the walls and ceiling, and I staggered, trying to swat them away.

"Maura!" Drew caught my shoulder, his hand as icy cold as mine. He might not have been able to see the ghosts, but he certainly felt their presence.

"The ghosts." I spoke through chattering teeth. "I don't know what's going on."

The air was thick with the dead. Debora watched wide-eyed from the corner of her cell as the door frosted over, ice spreading over the barred window. A torrent of cold air whipped through the cells like a hurricane, and a cracking noise reached my ears. My gaze snapped over to another cell, whose door had been torn clean off its hinges.

As its occupant stepped out, I tried to grab one of the ghosts. A jolt of icy cold seared my hand. They were *strong*, more than they should have been, and the rising wind caused both Drew and me to stagger sideways into the wall.

"What *was* that?" Drew asked.

"I don't know," I gasped in response. "I've never seen anything like this before."

I could guess *who* was responsible, but I'd never seen Hawkwood Hollow's ghosts demonstrate strength like this before. Gusts of icy air slammed the doors in their frames, and Drew uttered a curse when a second prisoner made her escape. This must have been even more confusing to his eyes than it was to mine. *What did Mina do?*

"Drew—be careful." I clung to the wall to keep from being

knocked over and began inching towards the door out of the jail. "I'll get to the bottom of this."

I emerged into the police station, which was in a similar state. Gusts of wind had swept reams of paperwork into the air, and officers ran left and right, trying to stop fleeing prisoners who I assumed had broken out of the holding cells.

"Hey!" I stuck out a foot and tripped one of Priscilla's allies. "What's going on? Is this your doing?"

"It's *her*," gasped the witch, whom I almost hadn't recognised without her pink hat. "She's coming!"

As she wriggled away from me, I took off at a run, following the fleeing ghosts out of the station.

Had Mina already performed her ritual? Whatever she'd done, the ghosts were fleeing in one direction as though they were being pulled by an invisible force. I debated following them, but first, I made for the cemetery.

As I'd expected, Harold stood outside his cottage, gripping his scythe. "You're too late, fool."

"What did she do?" I asked, my teeth still chattering. "Where are the ghosts going?"

"Your guess is as good as mine."

"Oh, come on. You must have some idea." I gasped again when another ghost floated straight through my body.

"Where's that brother of yours?"

*Mart.* "I left him with my mum. He's safe."

"Don't be so certain of that."

Alarm blared through me. I closed my eyes and reached out with my mind like I had the time I'd been trapped and drowning in the tunnel beneath Hawkwood Hollow.

*Mart,* I called out. *Mart?*

A moment passed before his reply reached me. *What? I can't believe you left me behind.*

*You're all right.*

*Why wouldn't I be? Why are you so cold, anyway?*

*The ghosts have all gone haywire*, I told him. *Something's dragging them across Hawkwood Hollow, and it started in the prison. Mina's allies are escaping, and whatever spell affected all the ghosts, I worried it got you too.*

*I can't leave you alone for five minutes, can I?* he replied. *I'll be right there.*

*No—wait—*

I opened my eyes to see a disgruntled Harold stalking past me with his scythe held aloft. "You shouldn't have called him here."

"You're the one who implied he was in danger." I shivered when another ghost floated past, joining the tide swarming down the street. "Where are they going?"

I peered into the afterworld, which was a lot easier in an open space than it had been in the cramped jail. The ghosts appeared to be converging on a spot somewhere outside the town's boundaries. Whatever it was, it had drawn all the ghosts like moths to a bright light.

As I made to step through the darkness to the source, Harold loomed over me. "Don't. Someone threw the equivalent of a bomb into the afterworld."

"Who?" Not Mina herself, surely. The sage surrounding the town would have prevented that demon of hers from getting inside—unless…

I turned back to the afterworld, focusing on the pulsing bluish light around which the ghosts circled like gulls. "Did you say a *bomb*?"

He didn't answer, but in a flash, Mart appeared at my side. "Hey, what's that shiny light over there?"

"It's a bomb, Mart," I warned. "If it goes off, I'm guessing it'll blow the afterworld wide-open and let Mina walk straight in."

"Correct," Harold growled. "I knew your pitiful barrier spells wouldn't be enough to keep Mina out."

"Thanks for the vote of confidence." I raised my voice over the roar of the wind and the collective murmur of a thousand ghosts being drawn towards the cold spot. The longer I kept my attention on the afterworld, the more deeply the chill worked its way into my bones.

Mart, by contrast, appeared to grow more and more solid the closer I moved to the glowing spot. Under the bright-blue light, Mart might have been the living sibling, and I looked more like the dead one.

"That's creepy." He peered at the spot of glowing light, which burned like a flame. "How do you defuse a magical bomb?"

"Very good question." The other ghosts circled the light, murmuring with awe, but even their solidifying hands passed straight through the bright spot. A faint thrumming in the air was the only clue that the light was anything other than benign. "I don't think we can."

I called the darkness to my numb hands.

Mart let out a gasp. "Maura… what are you doing?"

"Opening a door." It would have been easier with a scythe, but the afterworld answered my command regardless of the pulsing light blotting out my vision.

I closed my eyes and focused on the dark, on the world that awaited on the other side, deeper into the afterworld. *Come on.*

I heard Mart scream, and burning pain rippled through my entire body, washing away the numbness. I opened my eyes, seeing the light spot shrinking into the darkness of a door I'd opened beneath the bomb… and beneath me.

As I tumbled together with the bomb, arms folded around me, pulling me away from the door.

"Don't you *dare* go through there!" my brother yelled in my ear.

Then, his grip faltered, the brief strength he'd gained

turning to transparency once again. The door gaped open, threatening to pull me in. When I turned my head, I saw a shadowy figure, distinct against the darkness surrounding me. Tall, cloaked, and carrying a scythe.

Coming to collect my soul.

## 13

I watched the figure approach, my feet trembling on the edge of the abyss that awaited on the other side of that door.

"I told you," Mart yelled, "don't you dare die!"

The scythe-wielding figure loomed closer to me and to the roaring darkness without speaking. Under the Reaper's dark hood, I recognised his face. Dad.

"You can break the rules for her," Mart insisted. "Can't you?"

The door disappeared, and Dad sheathed the scythe over his shoulder and picked me up instead.

"Where is she?" I slurred. "Where's…?"

Mina. I figured he knew what I meant, but I passed out before I heard his reply.

―――

Some indeterminate amount of time later, my eyes opened, and I found myself lying in a bed that wasn't my own. The room was empty of everything but the most basic of furniture, and the walls were painted a dull beige. Curtains were pulled across the windows, but while curiosity stirred, I was too drained to cross the room and peer outside.

In the background, a blur of noise resolved itself into two voices arguing. Two *familiar* voices. My mum and dad.

*What?*

My mind went spiralling back a decade, and the pieces clanged into place. Dad hadn't taken me back to the inn but to the room at his old house where I'd stayed as a child. And it seemed my mother had realised I was here.

With a rush of adrenaline, I climbed out of the bed and tried to listen to what my parents were saying. Mum's voice was too high-pitched for me to make out the words, but I really hoped Dad hadn't told her I'd tried to defuse a magical bomb single-handedly. Or... well, anything else that I'd been up to over the past month.

*Here we go.*

I picked up my wand from the bedside table and pushed open the door, wondering where Mart had gone. He was probably hiding from our parents' argument.

My legs trembled, and I leaned on the wall to steady myself as I descended the staircase into the hallway. In the living room, my parents stood face-to-face, locked in a furious glaring contest.

Spotting me, Mum cried out, Maura!"

Sweeping across the room, she crushed me in a hug that didn't help my weary bones in the slightest.

Mart popped up. "Stop squishing her. She can't breathe."

I made a muffled noise of agreement. When Mum released me, I collapsed into a chair. This time, I hardly even noticed how uncomfortable it was.

"What... what's going on?" I looked between my parents, unable to process the dissonance of the pair of them being in the same house and not arguing... well, for the time being.

Dad had put down his scythe and hood and almost looked like a regular human, albeit a particularly pale and grumpy one.

"That's what I'd like to know," Mum said tremulously. "Your father tells me you fought a *demon* and nearly died."

I swivelled to Dad. "You told her?"

"I had to," he said without a hint of apology. "There was no other explanation for the state we found you in."

I looked down at myself. I was still wearing my crumpled clothes from the fight, but otherwise, I didn't have a scratch on me. "How long… how long have I been here?"

"Does it matter?" Mum asked with a sob in her voice. "I can't believe you risked your life like that and never even told me! I thought you were dying!"

"How long *have* I been here?" I looked between them, my heartbeat kicking up. "What day is it?"

"It's…" Dad paused. "The thirtieth of October."

"No." Halloween was *tomorrow*. "Mina…"

"Never mind Mina," Dad cut in. "You can't try a stunt like that again, Maura. I barely got you out of there in one piece."

"Would you rather Mina had blown open the afterworld on top of Hawkwood Hollow?" She'd almost succeeded in her plan, and with Halloween around the corner, she might not need a bomb next time.

"Blown open the afterworld?" Mum shrieked. "Who *is* this witch?"

"The former head of Hawkwood Hollow's coven." I didn't know what Dad had told her, but given Mum's agitated state, she probably hadn't taken in a word. "She made a play for power twenty years ago, when she used a ritual to summon a demon by flooding the village of Hawkwood Hollow and killing dozens of people. The local Reaper prevented her from bringing the demon into this realm, but she's been itching to try again ever since."

"The afterworld was damaged," Dad added, cutting through Mum's choked gasp. "The Reaper temporarily sealed the door, but that meant the ghosts in the town were unable to move on. Since then, there have been more and more spirits trapped in the town of Hawkwood Hollow, which has only made the afterworld more unstable."

"What kind of bomb was that, anyway?" I asked Dad. "It made the ghosts stronger… including Mart."

"What?" Mum wailed. "Mart? You knew about this too?"

"I didn't know Mina would drop a bomb on our heads," said my brother. "It was amazing. I felt like I could conquer the world."

"We don't need any of that," Dad said. "The bomb was formed of spiritual energy. Any ghost that went near the bomb grew stronger, but ultimately, they'd have been consumed."

"And the afterworld would have been ripped wide-open." I shuddered. "Where'd she get hold of a weapon like that?"

"At a guess, she built it with the instruction of her demonic ally," Dad replied. "I found evidence of several rituals in that house of hers."

"Crap." I thought back to my conversation with Debora Lowe. "Her former coven members escaped jail during the chaos. Have the police managed to catch any of them yet?"

I needed to call Drew. He'd be worried out of his mind, and so would Jia, for that matter. And Allie and Carey… "Where's my phone?"

"Oh, here." Mum reached into her pocket. "This is absolute madness, Maura. Rituals! Bombs!"

When she held out my phone, suspicion stirred inside me. "What were you doing with that?"

"Oh, I thought it needed an upgrade so that we don't lose contact again." She pressed the phone into my hand. "You weren't answering my calls."

"I was a little busy trying to defuse a magical bomb." I turned on the phone, groaning inwardly. She had changed the background to an old photograph of her, me, and Mart. Dad was not in the picture. My phone also showed dozens of missed calls and unanswered messages from Drew, Jia, Allie, and even Jennifer.

"I didn't *know* that, did I?" Mum choked out. "I had no idea."

"I didn't want to put you in danger." I saw Mart making gestures at me and recalled my promise to let our mother back into my life, but I'd intended to start on that *after* we brought Mina's plans crashing down. Not the night before Armageddon. "I'm sorry, but I need my phone to make sure my friends are still alive. Can you refrain from calling me every two minutes until after Mina is dealt with?"

Mum's face crumpled. "I just don't want to lose contact again. Is that so wrong?"

My insides twisted in knots, but I swivelled to Dad. "What *did* she do to my phone?"

"Set it to automatically answer all her calls, I think," my dad said apologetically. "I don't know. She claims she can help."

"With Mina?" I faced Mum again. "Not that I don't appreciate the offer, but I'm pretty sure only a Reaper can stop her at this point."

"Why on earth didn't you tell me?" Mum conjured a handkerchief and blew her nose. "If you'd asked, I could have used my own coven connections to find her."

"It's too late." Panic bubbled up in my throat. "It won't make any difference when we have less than a day until Halloween. She's already got everything she needs."

"To do what?" Mum waved her wand, and the handkerchief disappeared. "I don't understand what she stands to gain from this. Isn't she already coven leader?"

"Not since I drove her out of Hawkwood Hollow when I figured out that she'd been using her position to commit crimes."

"Despicable," Mum said. "A coven leader is supposed to protect her followers."

"Oh, she's never cared much for anyone other than herself," I said. "Even before she let herself get possessed by a demon."

"A *demon*." She shuddered. "Don't they normally kill their hosts?"

"We assume the pair of them came to some kind of agreement," Dad said. "That said, there's no telling if the demon will get the upper hand and finish off its host, and she's equally dangerous whether she's possessed or otherwise."

"Especially now she's let her allies out of prison," I added. "I guess Priscilla and her allies probably got out too."

"Priscilla?" Mum echoed.

"Another witch. Former coven member." I pushed to my feet, my legs shaky. "She offered to help us fight Mina and then changed her mind. One of her allies was the favourite to become coven leader before Mina snatched up the position."

Mum made a noise of disbelief. "Really. I thought some of *my* coven members were devious."

"That's why you deal with them before they can become a bigger problem," Mart interjected. "I told you."

Had he been giving her advice on how to handle our extended family? "Never mind Priscilla. We need to stop Mina from bringing in another bomb. We covered the entire town in sage and protective spells, but that wasn't enough."

"I told you," Dad said. "Sage won't be enough when the barriers between realms weaken."

"Then, what?" I challenged. "We're supposed to lie back and let her attack us?"

"No." To my surprise, he continued, "We set up an equally

strong barrier that will keep *anyone* out, human or otherwise."

My mouth fell open. "You're offering to help?"

He inclined his head. "I can't stop Mina single-handedly, but I can at least minimise the damage."

"You don't want her damaging the afterworld," I surmised. "Is that why?"

"That's not why." He took in a breath that he didn't really need, being a Reaper. "The town is important to you. Both of you."

Mart looked even more startled than I did and merely gaped at our dad, speechless.

Mum gave a prolonged sniff. "I can help protect you too. If you just *let* me."

"What do you want to do?" I asked. "Mina's possessed by a higher demon. Not much can defend against that."

"I know witches." She dabbed at her eyes with a handkerchief. "I'm used to dealing with scheming coven members."

She had a point there. "I don't want anyone to confront her alone. She's capable of anything."

Even if Dad and I managed to set up proper defences around Hawkwood Hollow, the afterworld as a whole would be unstable tomorrow, and Mina was unpredictable enough that I hadn't a clue what she might do next.

"My coven members can keep an eye out for any trouble," Mum offered. "Tonight is Samhain, you know."

"Yeah. I know. Tomorrow is Samhain…" I paused. "Wait. *Tonight?* You mean… it starts at midnight?"

"That's usually how days work," Mart said. "Oh. Oh, I see. Crap."

"Midnight," I repeated. "If it's true…"

That meant we had less than half a day to stop her.

## 14

I insisted on going back to the inn right away. Mum objected, claiming that I needed rest, but the notion of an imminent attack from Mina had momentarily washed away all tiredness from my body. It wouldn't last, I knew, but I needed to let Drew and the others know I was alive.

And I needed to do *something* to prevent Mina from attacking tonight.

I sent Mart ahead of me to pass on word to Jia that I was alive, and then I called Drew as I was leaving my dad's house. "Hey. It's me."

"Maura?" Drew's voice shook with relief. "Where *are* you?"

"Dad's house," I replied. "I'm on my way back now. Can you drop by the inn?"

I stepped into the afterworld and landed in the inn's lobby.

From behind the desk, Allie gave a gasp. "Maura!"

"Sorry I disappeared." I ducked into the restaurant.

Jia came running towards me. So did the other resident ghosts, who all tried to embrace me at once.

"Where'd you go?" Vicky asked. "We thought you left."

"Of course I didn't." I shivered, my human body objecting to being touched by so many ghosts at once. "I need to change into clean clothes. And shower."

"Me too," said Mart.

"No, you don't," Jia said sternly. "Give your sister time to get herself together."

"Fetch the Reaper," I told my brother. "Harold, I mean. He should probably be forewarned that Dad's coming to town."

"He is?" Jia stared at me. "Tell me all about it?"

"I will do." I managed to shake off the ghosts and returned to the lobby, where Allie was on the phone.

"Yes, she's alive," she was saying. "No—Carey, you stay at school. It won't be long until you can come home and see her."

"That's right." I raised my voice enough for Carey to hear me on the other side of the call. "I'm fine."

"See? No problem." Allie put the phone down. "Carey was distraught when you disappeared."

I winced. "It wasn't my plan. I'll explain everything as soon as I can."

I hastened upstairs to my room, where I took a quick shower and changed into clean clothes. By that point, my phone was buzzing again, and I had a new backlog of missed calls and messages. From Drew, mostly. From skimming through them, I gathered that he'd had his team searching for me as well as for Mina's escaped allies.

Allie waylaid me at the foot of the stairs. "Drew's here."

"Is he?" I spied him through the open door to the games room, talking to Jia. "Good. It'll be faster to explain to all of you at once."

"Maura." Drew raced over to meet me and swept me into

a hug. "I *knew* you must be alive, but my team couldn't find you anywhere."

"That's thanks to my dad spiriting me away," I explained. "I was knocked out cold, but I'm fine now."

"You must be starving," Allie said. "I'll get you something to eat."

"No, I will," Jia offered. "Mart already told me everything, about the bomb and the ghosts."

"The *what?*" Drew asked, aghast.

"It's not as bad as it sounds." I resignedly let him steer me towards the sofa at the back of the games room, around which the ghosts clustered as though contemplating my deathbed. "Mina tried to screw up the afterworld *and* create a diversion so that her allies could get away… Did they all escape?"

"Most of them did." Drew's mouth tightened in disapproval. "The team has been running around trying to find them, but we haven't had any luck."

"Have you checked Priscilla's hideout?"

"She isn't there," he said. "Mina must have swept in long enough to drive out Priscilla and her allies. We did manage to recapture some of *them*, but they're refusing to admit to having done anything wrong by trying to drive Jennifer away."

"Priscilla and her friends are too self-centred to be anything other than a liability," I said fervently. "As for Mina, I think that demon of hers taught her how to make a bomb formed of spiritual energy. She was trying to blow open a way into Hawkwood Hollow."

"What?" The colour drained from his face. "Please tell me you didn't pick up the bomb yourself. Is that how you nearly died?"

*Well…* "It's gone now, but Mina isn't, and we don't have long to keep her out."

"What do you want to do?" Allie pushed a mug into my hand. I sniffed, suspecting it was more of the same regenerative potion she'd given to me after my last fight with Mina. "We still have guests who will be arriving for the tour, but if you think she'll try to sneak in herself…"

"She won't," I replied. "She's possessed. Demons have a hard time with sage. You'll have to keep a close eye on the guest list, but I think Mina will try something more overt this time around. That's why my dad's coming to help."

I summed up the plan, as much as I understood of it, while Jia shoved a plate of food into my lap and all but forced me to eat. My phone buzzed continuously in my pocket, but since the settings Mum had installed didn't react and answer the call against my will, I could only assume that she was too busy to call me for once. Maybe Dad had told her not to disturb me.

When I'd finished eating, I fished out my phone and saw that most of the recent calls had come from Jennifer, of all people. Figuring she could wait, I put my phone away and resumed telling the others why I suspected Mina would attack earlier than we'd expected.

"Midnight!" Jia pressed a hand to her forehead. "I should have known. Why didn't I think of that?"

"I didn't either." I put my empty plate aside. "We've already set up enough defences around the inn, and the Reapers are on their way to help us strengthen security outside the town itself. Otherwise, keep an eye on the guests."

"A detection charm will help us make sure none of Mina's allies try to sneak in," Jia said. "I'll play security guard. Unless one of Drew's team wants to lend a hand?"

"Where is he?" Drew must have gone to take a call in the lobby. "Hang on. I'll talk to him."

I rose to my feet. My legs were a little shaky, but the

potion and food had revitalised most of my energy, and determination to stop Mina overrode any lingering exhaustion.

"Sorry," Drew said when I stuck my head out of the games room and spied him near the stairs. "They want me back in the office."

"Don't apologise for doing your job," I replied. "We might need your help, though. I don't know what kind of defences my dad plans on setting up—"

"Reaper!" someone yelped.

My attention snapped over to the door, where Harold had entered, carrying his scythe in both hands.

"Good, you're alive," he said.

"Good?" I echoed. "Was that sarcasm?"

"The town would be worse off if you were dead."

I blinked. "I'm glad we agree on one thing. Can you not wave that scythe around in here? It's freaking out the ghosts."

Several awkward minutes passed in which Allie and Jia tried and failed to make small talk with the grumpy Reaper, while the ghosts remained huddled in the corner of the games room. I urged Drew to go back to the police station, promising I wouldn't pick up any more bombs in the meantime, and waited for Dad to show up.

Typically, my father announced himself in his usual dramatic fashion, stepping out of the darkness and sending the ghosts fleeing in all directions. "Shall we begin?"

"You might want to explain what we're doing first," I replied.

"Show me where you sealed the afterworld, and I'll double the defences," Dad told Harold. "Then we can set up a spiritual barrier around the town."

"I'm guessing this is an experienced-Reapers-only thing?" I asked. "Because I'll help if I can."

"Stay here and protect the inn," growled Harold. "And let

your police know what we're doing so nobody gets in our way."

"All right." I sent a message to Drew and then examined my missed calls. "Why does Jennifer want to get hold of me so badly?"

"She was worried about you too," Jia told me. "She kept calling the inn when you were missing."

"She needs to worry about her own coven if you ask me." I shook my head. "Maybe this town doesn't need a coven at all. All attempts to form one seem doomed to failure."

"You aren't wrong." She hurried into the restaurant to take care of some customers.

I called Jennifer back. "It's me."

"Maura," said Jennifer. "I thought you were dead."

"Reapers are hard to bury. Don't you have a coven to run?"

"In a manner of speaking." Her tone was subdued. "The others are self-sufficient enough to keep running while I'm not present. The police have been reluctant to let me speak to Priscilla's allies, which limits my ability to plan for another potential coup."

"Never mind her," I said. "Worry about Mina. If she plans to strike when Samhain begins, that'd be midnight. Tonight."

Jennifer sucked in a breath. "What do you want me to do?"

Why did everyone keep asking me that question? "Find as many loyal witches as possible who are willing to fight, and bring them to the inn when I give you the word."

I ended the call and found my brother modelling his new Halloween lights, to the amusement of the people in the restaurant. Guessing that Jia had told him to keep them distracted, I flagged her down at the counter. "Do you need my help?"

"No." She shooed me away. "You need to conserve your

strength, not run around after the customers. I'm asking questions to make sure nobody here is Mina's ally, but it's tricky to do that without tipping anyone off."

"Yeah, you're better at diplomacy than I am." I ducked out into the lobby and found some customers of the transparent variety instead. "What are you all doing here?"

The ghosts had gathered at the foot of the stairs as though waiting for someone to meet them. I counted at least twenty, including the new ones who'd moved into the inn over the past few weeks.

"We want to protect the town too." Vicky drifted to the forefront of the group. "We want to help you."

"That's right," added Brian. "Hawkwood Hollow's our home."

"I know," I replied. "That's why the Reapers are setting up a protective shield around the town to stop Mina from getting in."

"We don't want to be trapped inside," said Jonathan. "We want to *fight*."

My lips parted when the other ghosts murmured agreement. I was hardly in a position to give orders when I had zero control over anything the ghosts did, yet they seemed to want my permission to act.

"If you want to fight..." I paused. "Ask Mart for the details. He'll be my representative for the dead."

As for the living, Allie had her wand out and was casting what I assumed were shielding charms over the doors.

"I'm going to close the restaurant this afternoon to everyone who isn't a guest here," she explained. "With the excuse that we have to prepare for tomorrow's tour."

"Yeah, I think that's for the best." If Mina struck tonight, the inn would be the last thing on anyone's mind.

"Oh... there's the coven leader." Allie lowered her wand and put it away. "Did you ask her to come here?"

"Yes, but not until we were ready to fight." I peered outside and saw Drew and his team approaching too. "I swear I didn't tell everyone to come to the inn right now."

Drew reached the doors first and entered, leading a team of officers that included, unfortunately, Petra. Behind him walked Jennifer and a small number of witches.

"What are you all doing here?" I asked.

"We were both walking in the same direction," Jennifer said, presumably to explain why they'd arrived at the same time.

"I thought it'd be easier if you explained to my team in person," Drew said apologetically. "I know the Reapers are helping protect the town…"

"They are," I confirmed. "They're setting up a shielding spell to stop the enemy from throwing any more magical bombs in here."

"Magical bombs?" Petra's voice was laced with disbelief. "I didn't see any bombs."

"Don't try to understand the afterworld, Petra," said Jia. "Leave this to the experts."

Petra looked affronted, but several of her fellow officers exchanged smirks. With narrowed eyes, she addressed me. "What does the *expert* have to say for herself, then?"

"If you want to help, you can keep an eye out for trouble around the town's borders," I replied. "We have until midnight before we really have to start worrying, but it wouldn't surprise me if Mina struck early."

"Midnight… why?" She sounded genuinely curious for once.

"Because it'll be Samhain," I said, conscious of the ghosts listening in as well. "The barriers between this world and the other side will be thinner than on any other day of the year. Mina intends to take advantage of that to call upon the forces of the dead to do her bidding."

My phone gave a loud buzz, and then Mum's voice rang out from my pocket. "Maura!"

Oh. Oh no. "I'll be right back," I told the mismatched group of ghosts and living and then ran into the games room to take the call. "Mum, I'm in the middle of something important."

"I had to call you!" She sounded frantic. "Some of my coven members have seen a group of strangers on the other side of Greenwood Lake, and one of them matched the description your father gave me of that witch you're chasing."

My heart jumped. "What... Mina Devlin?"

*Please, no.* If she'd figured out where my parents lived...

"I did as you said and didn't confront her," Mum said anxiously. "What should I do now?"

"Keep an eye out. I'll be there as soon as I can."

I ran out of the games room to find a sea of expectant faces.

"We have a problem," I said breathlessly. "I don't think Hawkwood Hollow is her target after all."

The doors slid open, and Dad and Harold entered. They were accompanied by Xavier, and the sight of *three* scythes sent the ghosts scurrying away to hide.

"Dad." I ran to his side. "I just got a call from Mum. She said her coven members saw Mina..."

"At Greenwood Lake," Dad finished. "I got a call from her too."

"Where?" Xavier asked. "I only just got here."

"Did your boss give you permission to come back?" I asked, secretly hoping he hadn't and that Xavier had had the nerve to defy him for once.

"He did," Xavier said. "I'm told you have a plan?"

"Not exactly." The lobby was awfully crowded by this point, and I was pretty sure some of the guests had got curious and come to eavesdrop as well. "Hey, everyone. There's been a change of plans."

My words only reached a handful of people, but Harold was on the case. The temperature dropped, shadows crept over the walls and floor, and silence filled the lobby. Nobody could kill a conversation more effectively than a Reaper.

"I'm pretty sure that Mina Devlin is targeting Greenwood Lake," I told everyone. "Those of us who want to fight her will have to leave Hawkwood Hollow."

"Are you sure?" Drew asked. "I thought she was fixated on this town."

"It's me she's fixated on." *And now she's gone after my family.* I should have guessed she'd try an underhanded tactic like that. "The inn will still need to be protected, but Greenwood Lake doesn't have any of our defences. I know your team will probably want to stay here…"

"I'll go with you." Drew's gaze was steady, his voice steely, certain. "Wherever you need me to."

"All right." I took in a breath. "Anyone who wants to fight can come with me. The rest can stay here and protect the town. That goes for everyone… living or dead."

This was it. Our battle with Mina was about to begin.

## 15

While Drew had been the first to volunteer to fight, Jia and Mart were next in line. The Reapers, too, except for Harold, who claimed he wanted to stay and protect the people of Hawkwood Hollow instead of coming with me to Greenwood Lake. Since he couldn't do that without a scythe, I hoped Dad had a spare one lying around somewhere.

Jennifer and some of the witches offered to come, too, but their numbers were paltry, and our small force would have little hope of overcoming Mina's in face-to-face combat. Hoping Mum would manage to convince some of her own coven members to help, I prepared to travel to Greenwood Lake.

Mart and I landed outside the Reaper's house, where our parents waited. Seeing Mum and Dad cooperating and not arguing was possibly the weirdest part of the whole thing.

"Where is she?" I peered downhill towards the lake.

"I think she noticed my coven members watching her," Mum replied. "I'm certain of what I saw, though."

Doubts began to stir, but I followed her lead towards the

lake. As we reached the shore, a torrent of sparks flew into the air like fireworks above the houses upon the island on the lake.

Mum halted, her face stark with horror. "They're on the island!'

*Oh no.* My brief hope that she'd been mistaken flickered and died.

Mum climbed into a boat, her wand in her hand, but I hung back and tapped into my Reaper senses. Now that she didn't have her anti-Reaper talisman, I thought I ought to be able to sense Mina's presence, but nothing leapt out at me from the afterworld.

"Did the demon kill her?" I whispered to Mart. "I can't sense Mina."

"Mina isn't here?" Drew asked, overhearing. "Is she going after Hawkwood Hollow while we're gone?"

"She might well be." That or she was hiding out of my sight.

"Sounds like her." Drew faced the lake, a growl building in his throat, but the only way for him to join in the fight would be to take a boat to the island himself. Was Mina somewhere over there, or was this a decoy?

"You want to go find her?" Jia asked me. "I guess without her anti-Reaper defences, you might be able to track her through the afterworld."

"You read my mind." I looked questioningly at Dad.

But he shook his head. "My place is here," he said. "I have to be ready to enact my duty as a Reaper."

Probably he meant that it was his duty to Reap the souls of anyone who ended up dying in battle. Panic spiked inside me. How could I leave my parents behind when they were under attack?

*Hawkwood Hollow needs me too.*

"I can help," Xavier offered. "But since I've never met her, I'll have to follow your lead."

"Same," said Jia.

"And me," added Drew. "I told you—wherever you need me to go, I'll be there."

"Yes, we get it, you're willing to die for Maura," Mart said helpfully. "Come on and get on with it."

"This is not the time for jokes." A torrent of firework-like spells sprayed out over the island, causing another bolt of panic, but Dad stepped between me and the island and looked me in the eyes.

"I'll make sure your mother is safe."

Oddly enough, I believed him. "All right."

I called the afterworld, taking Drew's hand in mine and reaching my free hand towards Jia's.

Then I fixed an image of Mina in my mind and stepped through the darkness.

My feet skidded on swampy ground. I looked up at Priscilla's magenta-painted house, no longer hidden by concealment and misdirection spells. Mina must have removed them... but why should she be here and not at her own hideout?

"Isn't this Priscilla's house?" Drew surveyed the building in surprise. "She's come back?"

"Apparently." I looked to Jia, whose brows rose. "Better tread carefully."

"Agreed," Xavier put in. "Ready?"

"I bet the door's Reaper-proofed." I used my wand instead, and the door sprang open. Gesturing to the others to stay back, I walked into the hallway.

In the room where I'd met with Priscilla and the others, Mina stood waiting for me. The floor had been cleared of the chairs that had been set out during my last visit, and nobody else appeared to be present aside from Mina. Oh, and the creature with which she shared her body.

"Maura." She gave the barest smile. "I expected you to come alone rather than putting your friends at risk."

"What are you doing, hiding here while your allies storm the coven in Greenwood Lake?" I asked. "For that matter, why'd you bother stealing Priscilla's hideout?"

"She and her friends defied me."

I gave a faint snort. "Do you actually have a plan, except for taking out everyone who defied you and ruling over the remains?"

The demon's voice spoke through her mouth. "I won't rule over a coven. My ambitions are wider now."

"Good for you." I narrowed my eyes. "What did you do with Shelton?"

"Oh, he's long gone," said the demon. "The afterworld appreciated my sacrifice."

"Sacrifice." My mouth went dry. As I looked into the demon's eyes, the darkness intensified as though I was staring into twin dark pits. "For what?"

Mina moved in a lunge that she surely hadn't been capable of before being possessed. I jumped aside but not fast enough to avoid being flung out of the room and into the hallway.

"Maura!" Jia caught my arm, steadying me.

"Don't get too close!" I warned, glimpsing Drew and the others out of the corner of my eye. "She's—"

Mina lifted a hand, but Xavier stepped between us, swinging his scythe. A huge furred shape leapt out of the air, throwing off his aim. *Not another of those monsters.*

"This is between me and Maura," Mina shouted, now sounding more like herself again. "You shouldn't get involved."

"As if you're known for playing fair." I couldn't beat her

alone. I was under no illusions on that front. "Nah, I'd rather cheat."

A second monstrous form appeared out of the air, mouth agape. I threw myself to the carpeted floor to avoid its jaws, which clamped shut perilously close to my head. *This isn't the place for a fight. I have to get her outside.*

I rolled to my feet and fetched up against the wall next to Jia. Through the open door, Mina stood in the spot where we'd met with Priscilla's allies, shadows spilling outward from her hands. With a demon on her side, she didn't need to be a Reaper for the afterworld to respond to her commands.

"Give up, Maura," said Mina. Or the demon.

Sparks flew past my face, and a new voice spoke. "Maura. Get out of the way."

I twisted around and saw Priscilla and the others approaching the house, wands in their hands.

"You're back?" Drew wouldn't be thrilled, but he could hardly haul them back to Hawkwood Hollow's jail when we were in the middle of a battle. "What, you want to fight her?"

"You don't know when to quit, do you?" Mina called to them. "Go away. This is between me and Maura."

"No." Priscilla pointed her wand at the house, sparks flying, but she and her allies made no move to enter.

Jia grabbed my arm. "They're going to blow this place up!" she hissed at me. "Get us out!"

The ground trembled underfoot, and I called the afterworld, seizing Jia's arm. She let out a strangled yell as I pulled both of us into the darkness, which deposited us several feet away.

Just as the building exploded in a torrent of smoke.

"Maura?" Drew started towards the building and then caught himself when he saw Jia and me lying in a heap on the grass. He ran to help me to my feet, keeping one eye on Priscilla and her allies. They stood in an arc, facing the smoke billowing out of the spot where the building had been.

"Did they just blow up their own hideout?" I'd left Xavier in there, but he was a Reaper, and even a building falling on his head wouldn't leave a scratch on him. I'd also lost sight of Mina behind the smoky haze.

"Apparently so." Jia was back on her feet, her wand pointed at the building. "I guess Isabella took Mina stealing her coven headquarters personally."

"You'd better not have freed any other prisoners," Drew warned the group of witches. "Or harmed any of my team during your escape."

"We didn't," said Priscilla. "We'll happily go back into custody when this is over."

"I think she's gone." Jia peered over at the house. "I don't see her."

"Has she gone to Greenwood Lake?" She would be either there or at Hawkwood Hollow, but her allies were at the former. "We'd better find her."

"I'm game." Jia nodded. "Drew?"

"Of course." His jaw tightened as he watched Priscilla conversing with her allies in a huddle, but he nodded. "Right. Let's go."

We stepped through the afterworld and landed beside Greenwood Lake. Dad hadn't moved from the bank, but on the island, sparks continued to fly from the windows, and I glimpsed Mum fighting alongside her coven members, her hair wild and her wand streaming a torrent of vivid blue.

"She's coming here!" I warned. "Mina is on the run. She'll attack either here or Hawkwood Hollow."

"I thought so," Dad said, displaying no surprise when Xavier appeared next to him.

"Sorry I left you behind," I said to the latter. "Did you see where Mina went?"

"I saw her grab a broomstick."

"Seriously?"

"What's going on in there?" Jia peered at the water, which had begun to shift around as though something unseen was stirring underneath the surface. Ripples spread outward, and the waters noticeably rose higher over the shore.

"The island!" Jia pointed across the waves, her expression horrified.

My heart lurched. The water level had risen high enough to wash the boats away from the shore.

There was no other way off the island. And we hadn't protected this town the way we had Hawkwood Hollow.

My mother came running out of the coven headquarters with her wand in her hand, shouting, "Stay away from my home!"

A torrent of sparks flew from her wand and into the lake. The turbulent waters began to calm, ripples smoothing out.

Drew swore, pointing upward. "There she is."

Sure enough, Mina hovered on a broomstick above the lake. She was too far away for any of us to reach, but even from this distance, I made out her expression of concentration as she pointed her wand down at my mother.

"No, you don't." I hopped into the afterworld and emerged in the sky, crashing into her broomstick.

I'd been hoping to knock her into the water, but she hung on tenaciously. Drew shouted my name as we bucked and tumbled in the air. A spell flew past, missing both of us; I caught Jia's frantic expression as she tried to aim at Mina without hitting me instead.

"What is it with you and trying to drown people?" I yelled in Mina's ear.

"It's a painless death." That time, it was Mina's voice that spoke, not the demon's. "More so than Shelton's."

*Shelton.* "What did you do? Offer him to whatever monster would do your bidding?"

"That's right," she said and threw me into the lake.

Or she tried. My Reaper talents kicked in, and I leapt into the afterworld before I hit the water. I landed on the shore next to my dad.

He turned to me. "What did she say?"

"She fed Shelton to—something in the afterworld." A sudden chill in the air made all the hairs on my head stand on end.

*What now?*

The waters of the lake had almost stilled, suggesting the danger had passed, but the chill indicated Mina had moved her focus to the afterworld instead.

"Where's she going?" Jia said. "She's flying away…"

So she was. Mina's broomstick had turned around in midair, while the waters of the lake stilled as she left them in her wake.

"I bet she's heading to Hawkwood Hollow." She clearly hadn't expected Mum's coven to put up a fight, and ditching her allies while they were losing a fight was just her kind of tactic.

"I'm guessing she is too," Jia said. "Let's hope those defences of ours hold up."

*I know.* I caught Dad's eye. "Do you have to stay here?"

"In case she comes back," he said. "But say the word, and I'll be right behind you."

"Thanks." I turned to Drew and the others. "Let's stop her."

The trouble with the defences we'd put up around Hawkwood Hollow was that they also prevented me from transporting myself directly into the town using my Reaper powers. Instead, I had to jump to the town's boundary—

taking Drew along for the ride—where I spied Mina's broomstick descending in a spiral over the river. A rush of satisfaction seized me when she stopped short in midair as she ran straight into the invisible barrier the Reapers had conjured up, though it was a shame she didn't lose her balance and fall in.

Spying me watching her, she veered over the grassy hillside.

"You can't keep me out of your town forever," she said, or the demon did. I couldn't tell whose voice was dominant at this point. "Samhain is mere hours away, and the afterworld itself already answers to my command."

Her feet touched down, and darkness rippled outward from her body as though she was a Reaper at the height of their power. A tremor of dread shook me. Was this all the demon's doing? Or was it Samhain being around the corner, thinning the veil, letting even a human like her access the afterworld?

Growling resounded within the darkness, and I spoke to my allies. "Watch out. She has more monsters."

"Figures." Drew spoke with a growl of his own. "I'll call the pack."

"What—?" I startled when he shifted into a werewolf there and then. I'd expected him to run back into Hawkwood Hollow to fetch his shifter friends, but instead, he let out a howl that I'd never heard from him before.

The pack's answering roar made even Mina's attention slip away from me as she looked for for the source. From the hillside, a furry mass of shifters ran to meet us, facing Mina's monsters without fear.

The resulting clash drowned out Mina's shrieked command, and more monstrous forms came out of the river of darkness: ghouls, shadow-beasts, and other monstrosities that I hadn't seen before. Even with the shifters Drew had

had waiting in the wings, there weren't anywhere near enough of us to fight off such a force.

*We can't lose.*

That was when the people of Hawkwood Hollow appeared on both sides of the river. Witches and wizards, shifters and other magical folk, forming a line between the enemy and the town.

Behind them were the ghosts. Hundreds of transparent forms rose on the horizon, ready to defend their home as well.

My momentary rush of relief was tempered when Mina stepped to the forefront of the darkness with a twisted smile that was far more demonic than human.

"I will not let you pitiful mortals thwart me!" shrieked the demon. "I will claim this town!"

"What do *you* have against us?" I asked of the demon. "It's Mina who has a reason to hate me, not you. You don't need to listen to her. I'm not even an official Reaper."

I stared into the demon's smoky eyes, and my brief hope of getting some understanding from the demon was instantly snuffed out when Mina's mouth curved into a smile. *I guess it was worth a try at negotiating.*

"As a Reaper, you are my enemy," said the demon. "But you're right… I'm strong enough now. I don't need her."

With a shock of icy cold, I felt the moment Mina's life was snuffed out. I stared into the dark, numb with disbelief.

After killing two Reapers, the demon had finally taken *her* as a sacrifice.

*Crap.*

My momentary shock subsided when the ghosts of Hawkwood Hollow rose up, forming a barrier around me.

But the demon merely laughed. "Your ghosts are pitiful compared to me. We'll see who breaks first."

The demon extended Mina's hands, and darkness spread

outward in a wave. I ducked, but the wave wasn't aimed at me.

Instead, her attack crashed into the barrier around Hawkwood Hollow. I held my breath, half-certain that the tidal wave of blackness would crash upon the houses—but the defences held, and a figure stepped to the forefront of the barrier.

Harold the Reaper.

"I banish you all!" he roared, waving his scythe. "Get out of my town."

His scythe parted the wave of shadows, which dissipated, but several of Mina's monsters took its place. Harold remained unperturbed, swinging his scythe in an elegant manner that I'd never seen from him before. It was a reminder that while he might look old, he was immortal, and he had been doing his job decades before I'd been born.

Yet the demon, too, stood like an ancient tree that had planted its roots deep in the earth. Unmoving.

"I will not bend!" the demon yowled. "I will not bow to any Reaper."

"You don't have a choice." Harold's scythe continued to swing, yet the monsters kept on coming, and the wave of darkness reformed itself every time he sliced through its shadowy crest.

From the barrier around Hawkwood Hollow, I heard an unmistakable crack.

*No.*

I leapt forward, running towards the demon, putting my body between the monsters and my home.

With a cry, Mart shouted, "Don't go near that thing!"

I planted myself in front of Mina's possessed body, heedless of the fresh wave of darkness rising in front of me.

"You won't survive the dark, Maura," said the demon.

"I'm a Reaper," I growled. "This is my domain."

"I know that, Maura Clarke," said the demon. "It's mine too."

"Don't be a fool," Harold shouted at me. "Don't give up your life."

"I'm not letting that demon through." I might not have had a scythe of my own, but the instant the demon broke through the barrier, the afterworld would break too.

"I can sense the power stirring below this town," the demon said. "Can you hold out that long, Reaper? Even you have a limit. Look at your friend."

My attention snapped over to my allies, but they were occupied fighting the monsters and had scattered all over the hillside. Then, my gaze landed on Harold. To my horror, his body had turned transparent, like a ghost. Had he put more of himself into that barrier than he'd let on, or was fighting the demon draining him that badly?

*He has a limit. Everyone does.*

Even the demon, who'd devoured the souls of two Reapers and who-knew-how-many innocent humans, had a breaking point. I just needed to find it.

"You don't belong here," I told the demon. "Get out."

"You know how to make it leave," Harold hissed at me, his body faded enough that I could scarcely make out his scowling face. "It's not really here, is it?"

"What does *that* mean?" Alarm stirred. He was fading away, and the demon advanced closer, a fresh wave of darkness rising at its command.

Except it wasn't the demon moving towards me, not really. The demon still clung to Mina's body. It wasn't fully in this realm.

Without stopping to think my plan through, I ran straight at the demon and jumped on top of it.

People have a tendency to stumble or collapse when

another person jumps on top of them, even if they're possessed by a demon.

And demons have a similar tendency to recoil when someone empties a packet of sage into their face.

Mina's body staggered, and the shadowy wave receded as the demon fought to push me away. When I lost my grip, a gleam caught my eye. The scythe arced through the air, and I raised my hands to catch it. I didn't need to look behind me to know that Harold was gone, that he'd thrown me the scythe in his last moment.

Then I brought the scythe down into Mina's body.

The demon's shadowy form rose like smoke, letting out a laugh. "You aren't a strong-enough Reaper for this."

"But we are," said Dad, and a dozen more voices echoed his words.

I stood stock-still, gripping the scythe in my shaking hands. Out of the corner of my eye, I saw Mart, his attention riveted on the robed figures drifting towards us past the remnants of Mina's army.

The Reaper Council.

# 16

The tall, hooded figures swept upon Mina's army, and a dozen scythes swung. They were efficient, I'd give them that, and I could do little more than blink in the time it took for Mina's allies to be swept away through the door of the afterworld. The demon, too, fell beneath their scythes.

Silence fell over the outskirts of Hawkwood Hollow. My allies gathered on the bank of the river, a mismatched group of living and dead, and despite my exhaustion, I felt a renewed surge of protectiveness towards them.

"Excuse me." I addressed the Reaper Council.

They ignored me. They were too intent on examining the protective shield around the town, gliding up and down the hillside and speaking in whispers too low for my human ears to catch.

"Hey." I spoke louder. "Can I help you with something?"

I didn't *intend* to speak with the authority of a Reaper, but some of that tone crept into my voice anyway, and it caused all the Reapers to stop their examination and swivel towards me like a row of puppets.

"Did you do this?" One of the Reapers gestured to the barrier.

"No." My heart stuttered. "Harold did. The local Reaper. He saved us."

He had too. It was just like the grumpy old Reaper to give up the last remnants of his life without warning any of us. Probably he hadn't even told Xavier. When I looked for the other Reaper, I spied a second hooded figure beside him.

*Mina's allies must have surrendered.* I tried to catch Dad's eye, but the Reaper Council descended upon him and Xavier without giving me a second's glance.

*Guess they'd rather talk to the proper Reapers instead of a half Reaper like me,* I thought with no small amount of relief.

As I ran towards my friends, Jia and Drew came to meet me—the latter still in his werewolf form—while Mart swooped ahead to join the other ghosts. A surprising number of them had left the safety of Hawkwood Hollow behind to join in the fight. To help me.

"Is she… gone?" Jia asked uncertainly. "Mina?"

"Yeah, the demon's gone," I replied. "Not before it killed Mina. She should have known that'd be the eventual outcome."

"Couldn't have happened to a nicer person."

Drew growled in agreement. He hadn't shifted into his human form yet, but in fairness, being naked in front of the Reapers probably wasn't appealing to him. Not to mention it was bloody freezing outside.

"Her body's somewhere over there." I pointed towards where she'd fallen beneath Harold's scythe. "I guess Mum and her coven must have got the upper hand on her allies for Dad to have come back here."

Drew growled again.

"I think that means he wants Mina's allies to be back in jail," Jia translated. "Not that I speak werewolf."

"Without Mina around, there shouldn't be any more jailbreaks." Though there was another group of witches to consider too. "What about Priscilla and her friends?"

Drew growled again, louder, which drew attention from the other witches.

Jennifer was amongst them, I noticed belatedly, looking somewhat windswept. When she caught my eye, she came over to meet me. "Maura, is she…?"

"Yes, she's dead," I said. "The Reapers took care of the demon. I don't know where Mina's allies are, but I'm guessing my mother's coven rounded them up."

"Your *mother?*"

"Didn't I tell you she was the leader of Greenwood Lake's coven?" I hadn't expected Jennifer to join in the fight at all—Wendy was noticeably absent—but I hoped that the other witches would appreciate that their leader was willing to fight on the front line to defend their town.

More people descended on me to ask questions, and it was all I could do not to tell them to go away. Half my attention was on the Reapers, whose conversation I couldn't hear from this distance and who might be discussing the fate of my home for all I knew. When Jia noticed my growing annoyance, she stepped in and shooed people away.

"She's exhausted," she said sternly. "We need to get back to the inn."

"I can't leave them out here without making sure they won't do anything to the ghosts." I indicated the Reaper Council. "Everyone else should go back into Hawkwood Hollow."

Most of the spirits had retreated, with the obvious exception of Mart. When I ducked over to him, I whispered, "Are you and the other ghosts okay?"

"Yes, but you're lucky not to be dead." He swatted me on the back of the head. "What did I tell you?"

"Old Harold is the one who gave up the most." He'd come through in the end, and I refused to let the other Reapers undermine his sacrifice in any way. "He wouldn't want the Council trampling all over the place."

"Go and wave that scythe at them."

"I highly doubt that'd improve the situation." Though I *did* have old Harold's scythe now, and nobody else was going to carry it. "Right. I'll see if they'll listen to me."

While the others had traipsed away—with the exception of Drew, who stuck behind me like a particularly large and furry shadow—I walked over to the Reapers and stood beside my dad. He glanced sideways at me, but his hood made it hard to see his expression. With a pointed stare at the Reapers, I held up my scythe. "Might I ask what you're discussing?"

"Where did you get that scythe?" asked one of the Reapers.

"Harold gave it to me," I told them. "I guess I'm the local Reaper now."

"You're human."

"Half Reaper." I jerked my head at Dad. "He's my father. There are no other Reapers in Hawkwood Hollow, and Harold gave me the job when he died."

He hadn't said so, but it was obvious that there were no other options.

The Reaper who'd spoken was silent for a moment before he spoke again. "A tear in the afterworld exists underneath this town. It's a nexus point."

"Yeah." My hands clenched around the scythe handle more tightly. "Harold sealed the afterworld to keep Mina's demon out. He didn't have a choice."

"Regardless," said the Reaper, "we can repair the damage. We will return after Samhain, when the barriers between realms are strong once again."

That should not have sounded as ominous as it did. And it shouldn't have been unexpected, either. There *was* a tear in the afterworld here. One that only the collective force of the Reaper Council could fix.

*But what if repairing the damage involves getting rid of the ghosts?*

---

After the Reapers departed, I had little choice but to return to the inn. Dad hadn't given me much more than a standard goodbye, but I gathered he was a little preoccupied with trying to keep the Reaper Council from entering Hawkwood Hollow there and then. Xavier too.

At the inn, the ghosts swarmed me at the entryway. Some wanted to cheer me as a hero. Others had more sober questions.

"Are the Reapers coming here?" asked Jonathan anxiously.

"I don't know." That was the honest answer. "Not yet. Not today. Nor tomorrow either."

"That gives us long enough to make a plan to send them packing," Mart said. "Should I call an emergency meeting?"

"No." I groaned, pressing a hand to my forehead. "We don't need to cause a panic. We've dealt with Mina. The Reaper Council is nothing in comparison."

I didn't think the ghosts were entirely convinced.

Luckily, at that moment, Allie and Carey came hurrying in from the back room. Carey flung her arms around me in a hug. "Maura! You beat her."

"I think the credit goes to old Harold, really." I let Allie hug me too. "And my mother's coven, for stopping Mina's allies. It was a group effort."

"Don't be overly modest," Jia said. "You nearly died for us."

"I'm fine." I glimpsed some of the inn's guests on the stairs, but they ducked out of sight when they saw me looking. "Has everyone been hiding in their rooms?"

"Yes," Allie said. "I thought that was the best way to protect anyone who was already here. I did offer them the chance to leave, but nobody took me up on it."

"Why?" I peered at the stairs. "What're they afraid of now?"

"Well, you are carrying a giant scythe," Mart pointed out. "Tell them it's a costume."

"Oh." I lowered my hands. "Yeah. I should probably see if Harold left a sheath somewhere in his house."

"Speaking of," said Mart, "are you going to live in his house now?"

"What?" I gave a choked laugh. "No. Of course not."

"Huh?" Carey blinked at me. "What's your brother saying?"

"He thinks I'm going to live in Harold's house."

"He's dead?" Carey's jaw dropped. "I thought Reapers couldn't die."

"He sacrificed himself for us," I told her. "And... and he gave me this."

She goggled at the scythe. "I thought you were just carrying it around. It's yours now?"

"I guess so." I stepped towards the stairs. "I'll stash it in my room. I won't be using it as a hat stand, though."

"You don't have to Reap ghosts now, do you?" Carey asked hesitantly.

"Definitely not." It didn't escape my attention that the ghosts shrank away from me at that question, Mart being the usual exception. "Come on, I'm not suddenly going to become a full-fledged Reaper. I didn't go to the trouble of keeping the Reaper Council out of town for all this time only to turn into one of them myself."

Not that they'd approved of my claiming the scythe. I almost hoped someone *did* cause trouble in the afterworld tomorrow and keep them away from here. Preferably on the other side of the country.

After I'd dropped the scythe off in my room, the other ghosts descended with more questions. Everyone seemed to want a piece of me, from the ghosts to the humans, and the guests finally came back downstairs and started bombarding me with questions as well. Mostly of the "is the tour cancelled?" variety.

"No!" I told them. "It's not up to me, anyway. It's up to Allie and Carey."

"And the ghosts," Carey added. "I... don't blame them if they don't want to go through with it after everything."

"Don't be absurd." I faced my brother, who'd donned his lampshade hat again, though he hadn't switched on the Halloween lights yet. "You want to go ahead with the tour tomorrow, don't you?"

"Obviously," he said. "We're not going to let the Reaper Council stomp in and ruin everything."

I repeated his words, and that was that.

---

I woke up on Samhain feeling surprisingly refreshed. It helped that I didn't have an upcoming magical battle with the forces of the dead on the horizon. Granted, I did have to wrangle the inn's ghosts into line for our upcoming ghost tour, but it didn't take much for them to get back into the spirit of things. Pun intended.

The guests were much the same. While they'd been understandably shaken by the outbreak of chaos yesterday, they'd stayed safely within the inn while all the fighting had been going on. I'd taken Mart's advice and pretended the scythe was a costume, though there was no way I was actually going to bring it with me that night. My job was supposed to involve staying in the background with Jia and Allie while Carey ran the tour.

I did not expect everyone to stare at *me* when I walked into the lobby while the guests were waiting for Carey to appear at the beginning of the tour.

"I knew I should have worn an unseen spell," I muttered to Jia as I joined her by the door. "They're supposed to be watching the ghosts."

"They will be," Jia whispered back. "You know… I think you *should* bring the scythe downstairs. Just for tonight. You don't have a costume."

Jia herself wore a zombie costume, complete with full makeup, and yet *she* wasn't the one being gawked at.

"What's that look for?" Mart zipped behind me, not yet wearing his own costume. "Why aren't you holding the scythe?"

"Not you too."

"Well, why not?" he challenged. "The ghosts aren't scared of you using it on them. What's the problem?"

I shrugged. "I don't want to take attention away from Carey and the ghost tour."

"You won't," he said. "*We're* the stars of the show tonight. I won't let them forget it."

"Exactly," Jia said. "Everyone knows you're the hero of the town—*and* you're the local Reaper. Why not give them this?"

Why indeed. Even after all this time, I hated being the centre of attention. Hated being noticed. It'd never brought me anything good in the past, and yet…

"If everyone's going to keep staring at me anyway…" I took a step towards the stairs. "I'll be right back."

When I returned to the lobby with the scythe, I was met with a wave of cheers. I halted, startled. When I saw Carey clapping, too, I hastened to step aside so that she could start the tour, but she shook her head and gestured for me to stay put.

"Welcome, everyone," she said into the microphone. "You might have noticed that we've had a bit of a disturbance over the past few days, but everything's fine now. It's all down to Maura here that the tour is going ahead at all."

More applause. I wished I'd worn a hooded Reaper cloak to hide my flushed face. That would have to be part of my next costume, assuming I made a habit of carrying the scythe around at all. Which was not the plan. Did I want everyone to recognise me on sight as the town's local Reaper?

Mart came to my rescue. Having donned his sparkly Halloween lights, he zipped in front of the crowd and bowed to everyone. That kick-started the ghosts' introductory routine, and I slipped away to join Jia while the others' attention was riveted on the inn's resident ghosts.

"See?" she whispered. "They might think you're a hero, but they paid for a ghost tour, not a Reaper tour."

To my astonishment, she was right. The ghosts kept everyone's attention for the full hour of haunting we'd promised, in which Jonathan treated everyone to a display of marching pumpkin-headed figures on the wall, while Brian dropped the temperature as a prelude to each new haunting. Wade and Louise rattled windows and doors to create creepy little tunes while the guests climbed the stairs to the upper level, where each room would contain a new spooky surprise.

Jia and I stayed downstairs to watch the door, though we didn't expect much trouble that night. In the end, the only person who showed up was Drew, a latecomer to the event, who greeted me with his customary hug.

"How's the tour?" He brushed a kiss across my lips, which I returned in kind.

"Good," I replied. "Really good. Everyone's behaving themselves, even Mart."

"And the Reaper Council?"

"Busy dealing with Halloween nonsense," I said. "You know, this is the night where a load of amateur would-be ghost hunters always come out and mess with the afterworld. The Reapers will have their hands full for a while."

"That's good." He smiled at me. "Hey... is that scythe real? Or a prop?"

"No... it's real," I said. "Mart and Jia wore me down."

"Damn right we did," Jia said. "She's the resident Reaper, right, Maura?"

I shook my head. "I won't be making a habit of this. Won't be moving into Harold's cottage either."

"I don't blame you," he said. "It's as cold in there as your dad's house. Have you heard from...?"

"My mum?" I guessed. "Yes, but she's been weirdly restrained today. I think she's been distracted by your team showing up to arrest those witches. It's good for her to have something useful to do."

I *had* promised to visit that weekend. I'd already given Mart my word, and besides, if I could handle fighting a demon, I could deal with my mother being more involved in my life. Dad too. I didn't need to worry about him reporting me to the Reaper Council. That was one silver lining of the situation.

"Speaking of witches," Drew said, "Priscilla and her allies have each given been a short jail sentence, but they'll be out by the end of the year. Is that okay?"

"Why ask me?" I queried. "I don't much care what happens to them."

"I figured, but I wasn't sure if you still held a grudge against them for their attempted coup against Jennifer."

"Does Jennifer?" I had my doubts. "It's not like they were all on Mina's side. I assume you hauled in her allies as well?"

"I did," he said. "That said, I'm in touch with the Wardens, and they've agreed to take her allies to a larger prison with more resources in case of another attempted breakout."

"I get the impression they couldn't organise themselves out of a paper bag without their leader." I wasn't too worried. "If they try anything, we'll stop her first."

---

The morning after Halloween, I went to check out Harold's cottage. I didn't particularly *want* to, but after Mart threatened to go in there without me, I reluctantly went along. Good job I did, because the first thing I saw was the Reaper-proofed ring that I'd taken from Mina lying on a shelf.

I picked up the ring with a faint shudder. "I think this needs to be handed to the Council. I'll give it to Dad."

He'd already told us that he'd retrieved Mina's book of dark magic, which she'd been carrying in her pocket when the demon had killed her. Her body, as far as I was aware, was the Reapers' responsibility. They wanted to make absolutely sure that her spirit never came back to haunt us.

"Told you it was worth searching this place." Mart floated over to an old bookshelf and blew a cloud of dust into my face.

I coughed. "Hey. Quit that... what, do you think there are more dodgy books in there?"

"No unofficial ones." Mart peered at the titles. "Hey... he *did* have a copy of *The Hitchhiker's Guide to the Galaxy*."

"Seriously?" I reached for the book, curious despite myself, and flipped it open. The front page read, *This book belongs to Rowan Wright.*

"I think that was his apprentice." I put the book back into

place, trying to tell myself that my eyes were stinging from the dust. "Is there a sheath for the scythe anywhere in here?"

It was weird thinking about Harold not being here. Weirder still that I held his scythe. I drew the line at wearing his cloak, though. I'd have to buy one of my own if I wanted to cosplay as a real Reaper.

My phone buzzed. Dad was calling me, and when I answered, he spoke nothing more than the cryptic sentence, "They're coming."

"I think he means the Reaper Council's coming here now." I'd expected as much, but adrenaline flooded me all the same.

Mart and I stepped through the afterworld and landed on the outskirts of Hawkwood Hollow, guessing correctly that they'd approach the town from the outside. I figured they'd want to look at the barrier again, and this time, they weren't held back by the dangers of meddling with the afterworld on Samhain.

Dad appeared first, a lone cloaked figure wielding a scythe. Then a dozen more almost-identical figures popped into view on the hillside. Facing them with only Mart at my side, I felt hopelessly outclassed.

"Hey." I injected as much confidence into my voice as I could muster. "What exactly are you doing here?"

"As we told you," said one of the Reapers, "we shall repair the damage that was done to the afterworld beneath this town two decades prior."

Tension gripped my shoulders. "You can do that? Without causing any more… ripple effects? Or blowing open the gates to the deeper afterworld?"

"Yes," said the Reaper. Judging by his voice, he must have been the same one I'd spoken to yesterday, but they looked far too similar for me to be certain. "Any ghosts who've been trapped here will be able to move on."

I fought the urge to look at Mart, but they didn't seem to have noticed him. As the Reapers converged into a group to whisper to one another, Dad moved to my side.

"It'll be fine," he whispered. "Harold's protections around Hawkwood Hollow are still intact. If they temporarily unseal the gate to the afterworld, the ghosts inside Hawkwood Hollow won't pass through to the other side. Not until the barrier is removed."

"They aren't going to take Harold's barrier down?"

He shook his head. "I convinced them not to, in the interests of safety. The barrier will keep everyone safe—including the ghosts."

"All right." I took in a breath and stood back to watch the Reapers work their magic.

Darkness clothed the world, turning the town into a dark mass and the countryside into a shadowy haze. The ghosts were visible as bright dots in the darkness, but a shimmering curtain encased them. Harold's barrier looked as solid as a physical wall from this angle, circling Hawkwood Hollow and protecting the entire town.

The Reapers swept towards the river. I might not have been able to see the gushing waters from within the afterworld, but I was familiar enough with the layout to know where the Reapers were going. They descended straight through what in the real world was solid ground, covering the tunnels. Mina's underground hideout had been closed off, but no physical barrier could keep out a Reaper.

Curiosity seized me. Stepping into the darkness, I followed the Reapers downward through solid earth. They'd come to a halt before what I could only describe as a gate, though it was as shimmering and indistinct as a door through which ghosts passed, never to return. At first, it was like looking down at the surface of a murky lake and seeing the indistinct reflection of a gate, but the longer I looked, the more details leapt out. The gate's halves fit together at crooked angles, interlocked chains holding them closed.

"Shelton did that." I spoke to Mart more than to the Reapers; they paid me no more attention than they would a smear on the wall. They'd gathered around the gates, exchanging whispers.

I didn't *see* what they did, but I sure felt it. A vibration shook the entire afterworld, and Mart grabbed onto me with a yelp. "Don't let me go."

"I won't," I murmured. "Hold onto me. It'll be okay."

More reverberations shook the afterworld as the chains holding the gates closed vanished with scarcely a whisper. The gates began to open, but the Reapers moved into the way, forming a shadowy barrier to the other side.

Mart and I clung to one another as the vibration quietened and then ceased. The Reapers moved to either side, revealing nothing but darkness where the gate had previously stood.

Finally, one of them spoke to me. "You shouldn't have followed."

"I had to see." I still held onto my brother, defiant. "This town is important to me. Is… is it fixed? The afterworld."

"It is done." Without another word, they swept upward as one.

Not wanting to linger, Mart and I followed. We landed on the shore of the river, where the shadows receded, and the ground turned reassuringly solid underfoot.

"Now, you will act as Reaper for this region?" asked one of them.

It took me a moment to realise he was talking to Dad, not to me. My father apparently hadn't been curious enough to go watch the Reapers seal the afterworld, and his moment of hesitation suggested the question had taken him by surprise too.

"That's not necessary," he replied. "My daughter has already been chosen as Reaper by her predecessor."

"She's mortal."

*Like that's a bad thing.* "I have a long life ahead of me. Maybe another Reaper will come along. Maybe I'll take on an apprentice. You can leave us alone for the time being, can't you?"

Instead of replying to me, the Reapers converged into a huddle again. Dad moved in to talk to them, too, and Mart and I were shut out of the circle. *That* was familiar.

"They'll have to say yes," my brother said. "You're the only person available *and* willing to do the job. Besides, you can chase them off with your scythe if they say no."

"I highly doubt that would help." Sure was tempting, though. What right did these people have to barge into Hawkwood Hollow and start remaking the rules after ignoring the town's existence for decades? They hadn't even checked up on Harold or comforted him after he'd lost his apprentice. Reapers might pretend to be unfeeling, but they weren't, and I knew Harold had grieved for years. Just like Dad had for Mart.

The Reapers' whispers petered out, and Dad approached Mart and me alone. "Good news."

My heart leapt. "They said yes?"

"They did," Dad confirmed. "I suspect they'll want me to periodically check up on you, but otherwise, are you sure you want to do this? Banishing ghosts isn't an easy job."

"I know." I'd been doing it for years, long after I'd supposedly given up on being a Reaper. "It's a small town. I'll manage."

I didn't say the obvious—I didn't *have* to banish every ghost—but that must have been on his mind.

"Good," he said. "Ah… the defences around Hawkwood Hollow won't last forever. I believe Harold only intended for them to stay long enough to ensure the Council didn't accidentally cause any damage when they inevitably showed up to help."

"I figured." I slid a hand into my pocket and pulled out the ring. "Do you want to take this? It's Mina's. I think she made it herself."

"Her Reaper-proof talisman?" He held out a hand for it. "Yes… the Council will want to study this. Working out where it came from ought to keep them occupied for a bit."

"Thought so," I replied. "I'll see you at the weekend? I promised I'd drop in and visit Mum. I want to make sure everyone's okay after her coven was attacked."

"I think they are," Dad replied. "I also think certain extended family members of yours have been less insistent about her incompetence after that incident."

"Good." I allowed myself a grin. "They'll have a hard time unseating her now."

There was still the matter of the coven's succession, but Mum must know by now that I wasn't the person—or Reaper—for the job.

After we'd parted ways with Dad and the Reaper Council had departed, Mart and I returned to the inn. As I'd expected, the ghosts instantly swarmed us at the entryway.

"Is this it?" asked Vicky tremulously. "Are the Reapers coming here?"

"No." I faced the audience of anxious spirits. "They repaired the damage that Mina initially did to the afterworld, but otherwise, I'm in charge of any banishments, and I swear I won't send any ghost to the next world who doesn't want to leave."

Cheers rang out. The ghosts rattled the doors in celebration, making such a racket that Allie and Carey came out of the restaurant to see what was going on.

"The Reapers have repaired the damage," I told them. "The ghosts are safe. Unless they *want* to move on...?"

"No way," said Mart. "We're staying here. Right?"

The other ghosts echoed the call. I blinked back unexpected tears, which made my brother laugh.

"See, she's a huge softie at heart," said Mart. "She'll be the first official Reaper to never banish anyone, mark my words."

"But..." Carey began. "If you're the official Reaper, are you still going to be able to help with the ghost tours?"

"Of course." I grinned at my friends, at my family. "I wouldn't be anywhere else. I'm staying in Hawkwood Hollow."

Dead or living, the town was my home. I'd defend it with everything I had. And I had the scythe to prove it.

## ABOUT THE AUTHOR

Elle Adams lives in the middle of England, where she spends most of her time reading an ever-growing mountain of books, planning her next adventure, or writing. Elle's books are humorous mysteries with a paranormal twist, packed with magical mayhem.

She also writes urban and contemporary fantasy novels as Emma L. Adams.

Find out more about Elle's books at: https://www.elleadamsauthor.com/

Find Elle on Facebook at https://www.facebook.com/pg/ElleAdamsAuthor/

www.ingramcontent.com/pod-product-compliance
Lightning Source LLC
LaVergne TN
LVHW041635060526
838200LV00040B/1581